Margaret Oliphant

A Country Gentleman and his Family

Volume 1

Margaret Oliphant

A Country Gentleman and his Family
Volume 1

ISBN/EAN: 9783337230753

Printed in Europe, USA, Canada, Australia, Japan

Cover: Foto ©Andreas Hilbeck / pixelio.de

More available books at **www.hansebooks.com**

A COUNTRY GENTLEMAN

AND HIS FAMILY

BY

MRS. OLIPHANT

AUTHOR OF 'THE WIZARD'S SON,' 'HESTER,' ETC.

IN THREE VOLUMES

VOL. I.

London

MACMILLAN AND CO.

1886

A COUNTRY GENTLEMAN.

CHAPTER I.

THEODORE WARRENDER was still at Oxford when his father died. He was a youth who had come up from his school with the highest hopes of what he was to do at the university. It had indeed been laid out for him by an admiring tutor with anticipations which were almost certainties : " If you will only work as well as you have done these last two years !" These years had been spent in the dignified ranks of Sixth Form, where he had done almost everything that boy can do. It was expected that the School would have had a holiday when he and Brunson went up for the scholarships in their chosen college, and everybody calculated on the " double event." Brunson got the scholarship in question, but Warrender failed, which at first astonished everybody, but was afterwards more than accounted for by the fact that his fine and fastidious mind had been carried away by the Æschylus paper, which he made into an ex-

haustive analysis of the famous trilogy, to the neglect of
other less inviting subjects. His tutor was thus almost
more proud of him for having failed than if he had succeeded, and Sixth Form in general accepted Brunson's
success apologetically as that of an "all-round" man, whose
triumph did not mean so much. But if there is any place
where the finer scholarship ought to tell, it should be in
Oxford, and his school tutor, as has been said, laid out for
him a sort of little map of what he was to do. There were
the Hertford and the Ireland scholarships, almost as a
matter of course; a first in moderations, but that went
without saying; at least one of the Vice-Chancellor's prizes
—probably the Newdigate, or some other unconsidered
trifle of the kind; another first class in Greats; a fellow-
ship. "If you don't do more than this I will be disappointed
in you," the school tutor said.

The college tutors received Warrender with suppressed
enthusiasm, with that excitement which the acquisition of a
man who is likely to distinguish himself (and his college)
naturally calls forth. It was not long before they took his
measure and decided that his school tutor was right. He
had it in him to bring glory and honour to their doors.
They surrounded him with that genial warmth of incubation
which brings a future first class tenderly to the top of
the lists. Young Warrender was flattered, his heart was

touched. He thought, with the credulity of youth, that the dons loved him for himself; that it was because of the attractions of his own noble nature that they vied with each other in breakfasting and dining him, in making him the companion of their refined and elevated pleasures. He thought, even, that the Rector—that name of fear—had at last found in himself the ideal which he had vainly sought in so many examples of lettered youth. He became vain, perhaps, but certainly a little self-willed, as was his nature, feeling himself to be on the top of the wave, and above those precautions for keeping himself there which had once seemed necessary. He did not, indeed, turn to any harm, for that was not in his nature; but feeling himself no longer a schoolboy, but a man, and the chosen friend of half the dons of his college, he turned aside with a fine contempt from the ordinary ways of fame-making, and betook himself to the pursuit of his own predilections in the way of learning. He had a fancy for out-of-the-way studies, for authors who don't pay, for eccentricities in literature; in short, for having his own way and reading what he chose. Signals of danger became gradually visible upon his path, and troubled consultations were held over him in the common room. " He is paying no attention to his books," remarked one; "he is reading at large whatever pleases him." Much was to be said for this principle, but still, alas, these gentlemen were all agreed that it does not pay.

"If he does not mind, he will get nothing but a pass," the Rector said, bending his brows. The learned society shrank, as if a sentence of death had been pronounced.

"Oh no, not so bad as that!" they cried, with one voice.

"What do you call so bad as that? Is not a third worse than that? Is not a second quite as bad?" said the majestic presiding voice. "In the gulf there are no names mentioned. We are not credited with a mistake. It will be better, if he does not stick to his books, that he should drop."

Young Warrender's special tutor made frantic efforts to arrest this doom. He pointed out to the young man the evil of his ways. "In one sense all my sympathies are with you," he said; "but, my dear fellow, if you don't read your books you may be as learned as ———, and as clear-sighted as ———" (the historian, being unlearned, does not know what names were here inserted), "but you will never get to the head of the lists, where we have hoped to see you."

"What does it matter?" said Warrender, in boyish splendour. "The lists are merely symbols. You know

one's capabilities without that ; and, as for the opinion of
the common mass, of what consequence is it to me ?"

A cold perspiration came out on the tutor's brow. " It
is of great consequence to—the college," he said. " My
dear fellow, so long as we are merely mortal we can't
despise symbols ; and the Rector has set his heart on having
so many first classes. He doesn't like to be disappointed.
Come, after it's all over you will have plenty of time to
read as you like."

" But why shouldn't I read as I like now ?" said Warrender. He was very self-willed. He was apt to start off at
a tangent if anybody interfered with him,—a youth full of
fads and ways of his own, scorning the common path,
caring nothing for results. And by what except by results
is a college to be known and assert itself? The tutor
whose hopes had been so high was in a state of depression
for some time after. He even made an appeal to the
school tutor, the enthusiast who had sent up this troublesome original with so many fine prognostications : who
replied to the appeal, and descended one day upon the
youth in his room, quite unexpectedly.

" Well, Theo, my fine fellow, how are you getting on ?
I hope you are keeping your eyes on the examination, and
not neglecting your books."

" I am delighted to see you, sir," said the lad. " I was

just thinking I should like to consult you upon"—and here he entered into a fine question of scholarship,—a most delicate question, which probably would be beyond the majority of readers, as it is of the writer. The face of the public-school man was a wonder to see. It was lighted up with pleasure, for he was an excellent scholar, yet clouded with alarm, for he knew the penalties of such behaviour in a "man" with an examination before him.

"My dear boy," he said, "in which of your books do you find any reference to that?"

"In none of them, I suppose," said the young scholar. "But, you don't think there is any sanctity in a set of prescribed books?"

"Oh no, no sanctity: but use," said the alarmed master. "Come, Theo, there's a good fellow, don't despise the tools we all must work with. It's your duty to the old place, you know, which all these newspaper fellows are throwing stones at whenever they have a chance: and it's your duty to your college. I know what you are worth, of course: but how can work be tested to the public eye except by the lists?"

"Why should I care for the public eye?" said the magnanimous young man. "*We* know that the lists don't mean everything. A headache might make the best scholar that ever was lose his place. A fellow that knows nothing

might carry the day by a fluke. Don't you remember, sir,
that time when Daws got the Lincoln because of that old
examiner, who gave us all his own old fads in the papers?
Every fellow that was any good was out of it, and Daws
got the scholarship. I am sure you can't have forgotten
that."

"Oh no, I have not forgotten it," said the master
ruefully. "But that was only once in a way. Come,
Theo, be reasonable. As long as you are in training, you
know, you must keep in the beaten way. Think, my boy,
of your school—and of me, if you care for my credit as
a tutor."

"You know, sir, I care for you, and to please you,"
said Warrender, with feeling. "But as for your credit as
a tutor, who can touch that? And even I am not unknown
here," he added, with a little boyish pride. "Everybody
who is of any importance knows that the Rector himself
has always treated me quite as a friend. I don't think"
—this with the ineffable simple self-assurance of youth, so
happy in the discrimination of those who approve of it that
the gratification scarcely feels like vanity—"that I shall be
misunderstood here."

"Oh, the young ass!" said the master to himself, as he
went away. "Oh, the young idiot! Poor dear Theo,
what will be his feelings when he finds out that all they

care for is the credit of the college?" But he was not so
barbarous as to say this, and Warrender was left to find
out by himself, by the lessening number of the breakfasts,
by the absence of his name on the lists of the Rector's
dinner-parties, by the gradual cooling of the incubating
warmth, what had been the foundation of all the affection
shown him. It was not for some time that he perceived
the change which made itself slowly apparent, the gradual
loss of interest in him who had been the object of so much
interest. The nest was, so to speak, left cold, no father
bird lending his aid to the development; his books were
no longer forced on his consideration; his tutor no longer
made anxious remarks. Like other silly younglings, the
lad for a while rejoiced in his freedom, and believed that
he had succeeded in making his pastors and teachers aware
of a better way. And it was not till there flashed upon
him the awful revelation that *they were taking up Brunson*,
that he began to see the real state of affairs. Brunson was
the all-round man whom Sixth Form despised,—a fellow
who had little or no taste for the higher scholarship, but
who always knew his books by heart, mastering everything
that would "pay" with a determined practical faculty fertile
of results. There is no one for whom the dilettante mind
has a greater contempt; and when Warrender saw that
Brunson figured at the Rector's dinner-parties as he him-

self had once done, that it was Brunson who went on the river with parties of young dons and walked out of college arm in arm with his tutor, the whole meaning of his own brief advancement burst upon him. Not for himself, as he had supposed in the youthful simplicity which he called vanity now, and characterised by strong adjectives; not in the least for him, Theo Warrender, scholar and gentleman, but for what he might bring to the college,—the honours, the scholarships, the credit to everybody concerned in producing a successful student. That he became angry, scornful, and Byronic on the spot need surprise nobody. Brunson! who never had come within a hundred miles of him or of his set at school; did not even understand the fine problems which the initiated love to discuss; was nothing but a plodding fellow, who stuck to his work, and cared no more for the real soul of Greek literature or philosophy than the scout did. Warrender laughed aloud,—that hollow laugh, which was once so grand an exponent of feeling, and which, though the Byronic mood has gone out of fashion, will never go out of fashion so long as there is youthful pride to be wounded, and patient merit has to accept the spurns of the unworthy. No, perhaps the adjective is mistaken, if Shakespeare ever was mistaken; not patient, but exasperated merit, conscious to the very finger points of its own deserts.

Warrender was well enough aware that he could, if he chose, make up the lost way and leave Brunson "nowhere" in the race for honours; but it was his first disenchantment, and he felt it deeply.   Letters are dear and honours sweet, but our own beloved personality is dearer still; and there is no one who does not feel humbled and wounded when he finds out that he is esteemed, not for himself, but for what he can do,—and poor Theo was only twenty, and had been made much of all his life.   He began to ask himself, too, whether his past popularity, the pleasant things that had been always said of him, the pleasant way in which his friendship had been sought, were perhaps all inspired by the same motive,—because he was likely to do credit to his belongings and friends.   It is a fine thing to do credit to your belongings, to be the pride of your community, to be quoted to future generations as the hero of the past. This was what had occurred to him at school, and he had liked it immensely.   Warrender had been a word to conjure withal, named by lower boys with awe, fondly cherished in the records of Sixth Form.   But the glimmer in the Head Master's eye as he said good-bye, the little falter in his tutor's voice,—did these mean no more than an appreciation of his progress, and an anticipation of the honour and glory he was to bring them at the university, a name to fling in the teeth of the newspaper fellows next time they demanded what were the results of the famous public school system? This thought had a sort of maddening effect upon the fastidious, hot-headed, impatient young man. He flung his books into a corner of the room, and covered them over with a yellow cairn of railway novels. If that was all, there let them lie. He resolved that nothing would induce him to touch them more.

The result was—but why should we dwell upon the result? It sent a shiver through the college, where there were some faithful souls who still believed that Warrender could pick up even at the last moment, if he liked. It produced such a sensation in his old school as relaxed discipline entirely, and confounded masters and scholars in one dark discouragement. "Warrender has only got a —— in Mods." We decline to place any number where that blank is; it filled every division (except the lowest) with consternation and dismay. Warrender! who was as sure of a first as—why, there was nobody who was so sure as Warrender! The masters who were Cambridge men recovered their courage after a little, and said, "I told you so! That was a boy who ought to have gone to Cambridge, where individual characteristics are taken into consideration." Warrender's tutor took to his bed, and was not visible for a week, after which only the most unsympathetic, not to say brutal, of his colleagues would have mentioned before

him Warrender's name.   However, time reconciles all
things, and after a while the catastrophe was forgotten and
everything was as before.

But not to Warrender himself.   He smiled, poor boy,
a Byronic smile, with a curl of the upper lip such as suited
the part, and saw himself abandoned by the authorities
with what he felt to be a lofty disdain ; and he relapsed
into such studies as pleased him most, and set prescribed
books and lectures at defiance.   What was worst to bear
was that other classes of " men " made up to him, after the
men of distinction, those whom the dons considered the
best men, had withdrawn and left him to pursue his own
way.   The men who loafed considered him their natural
prey ; the æsthetic men who wrote bad verses opened their
arms, and were ready to welcome him as their own.   And
perhaps among these classes he might have found disin-
terested friendship, for nobody any longer sought Warrender
on account of what he could do.   But he did not make the
trial, wrapping himself up in a Childe-Harold-like superiority
to all those who would consort with him, now that he had
lost his hold of those with whom only he desired to consort.
His mother and sisters felt a little surprised, when they
came up to Commemoration, to find that they were not
overwhelmed by invitations from Theo's friends.   Other
ladies had not a spare moment : they were lost in a tur-

moil of breakfasts, luncheons, water-parties, concerts, flower-
shows, and knew the interior of half the rooms in half the
colleges. But with the Miss Warrenders this was not so.
They were asked to luncheon by Brunson, indeed, and had
tea in the rooms of a young Cavendish, who had been at
school with Theo. But that was all, and it mortified the
girls, who were not prepared to find themselves so much
at a disadvantage. This was the only notice that was
taken of his downfall at home, where there was no
academical ambition, and where everybody was quite satisfied so long as he kept his health and did not get into
any scrape. Perhaps this made him feel it all the more,
that his disappointment and disenchantment were entirely
shut up in his own bosom, and that he could not confide
to any one the terrible disillusionment that had befallen
him on the very threshold of his life. That the Rector
should pass him with the slightest possible nod, and his
tutor say " How d'ye do, Warrender ?" without even a smile
when they met, was nothing to anybody except himself.
Arm in arm with Brunson, the don would give him that
salutation. Brunson, who had got his first in Mods, and
was going on placidly, admired of all, to another first in
the final schools.

But if there was any one who understood Warrender's
feelings it was this same Brunson, who was in his way an

honest fellow, and understood the situation. "It is all pot-hunting, you know," this youth said. "They don't care for me any more than they care for Jenkinson. It's all for what I bring to the college, just as it was for what they ex-pected you were going to bring to the college; only I understood it, and you didn't. I don't care for them any more than they do for me. Why, they might see, if they had any sense, that to work at you, who care for that sort of thing, would be far better than to bother me, who only care for what it will bring. If they had stuck to you they might have done a deal with you, Warrender: whereas I should have done just the same whether they took any notice of me or not."

"You mean to say I'm an empty-headed fool that could be cajoled into anything!" cried the other angrily.

"I mean nothing of the sort. I mean that I'm going to be a schoolmaster, and that first classes, etc., are my stock in trade. You don't suppose I work to please the Rector? And I know, and he knows, and you know, that I don't know a tenth part so much as you do. If they had held on at you, Theo, they might have got a great scholar out of you. But that's not what they want. They want so many firsts, and the Hertford, and the Ireland, and all the rest of it. It's all pot-hunting," Mr. Brunson said. But this did not lessen the effect of the disenchantment, the first disappointment of life. Poor Theo became prone to suspect everybody after that first proof that no one was above suspicion,—not even the greatly respected head of one of the first colleges in the world.

After that dreadful fiasco in the schools, Warrender continued to keep his terms very quietly; seeing very few people, making very few friends, reading after his own fashion with an obstinate indifference to all systems of study, and shutting his eyes persistently to the near approach of the final ordeal. Things were in this condition when he received a sudden telegram calling him home. "Come at once, or you will be too late," was the message. The Rector, to whom he rushed at once, looked at it coldly. He was not fond of giving an undergraduate leave in the middle of the term. "The college could have wished for a more definite message," he said. "Too late for what, Mr. Warrender?" "Too late to see my father alive, sir!" cried the young man; and as this had all the definiteness that the college required he was allowed to go. This was how his studies were broken up just as they approached their conclusion, although, as he had been so capricious and self-willed, nobody expected that in any circumstances it could have been a very satisfactory close.

CHAPTER II.

THE elder Mr. Warrender was a country gentleman of an undistinguished kind. The county gentry of England is a very comprehensive class. It includes the very best and most delightful of English men and English women, the truest nobility, the finest gentlemen; but it also includes a number of beings the most limited, dull, and commonplace that human experience knows. In some cases they are people who do well to be proud of the generation of gentlefolk through whom they trace their line, and who have transmitted to them not only the habit of command, but the habit of protection, and that easy grace of living which is not to be acquired at first hand; and there are some whose forefathers have handed down nothing but so many farms and fields, and various traditions, in which father and son follow each other, each smaller and more petty of soul than he that went before. The family at the Warren were of this class. They were acknowledged gentry, beyond all question, but their estates and means were small and their souls smaller. Their income never reached a higher level than about fifteen hundred a year. Their paternal home was a house of rather mean appearance, rebuilt on the ruins of the old one in the end of last century, and consequently as ugly as four square walls could be. The woods had grown up about it, and hid it almost entirely from sight, which was an advantage, perhaps, to the landscape, but not to those who were condemned to dwell in the house, which was without light and air and everything that was cheering. The name of the Warren was very well adapted to the place, which, except one corner of the old house which had stood fast when the rest was pulled down, might almost have been a burrow in the soft green earth, damp and warm and full of the mould of ages, though it was a mere new-comer in the world. Its furniture was almost entirely of the same date as the house, which means dingy carpets, curtains of harsh and unpliable stuff, and immense catafalques of mahogany in the shape of sideboards, arm-chairs, and beds. A four-poster of mahogany, with hangings of red moreen, as stiff as a board and much less soft,—that was the kind of furnishing; to be sure, it was full of feather-beds and pillows, warm blankets and fresh linen, which some people thought made amends.

The family consisted of Mr. and Mrs. Warrender, two daughters, and the son, with whom the reader has already made acquaintance. How he had found his way into such a nest was one of those problems which the prudent evolutionist scarcely cares to tackle. The others were in their natural place : the father a Warrender like the last dozen Warrenders who had gone before him, and the girls cast exactly in the mould of all the previous Minnies and Chattys of the family. They were all dull, blameless, and good—to a certain extent; perfectly satisfied to live in the Warren all the year long, to spend every evening of their lives round the same hearth, to do the same thing to-day as they had done yesterday and should do to-morrow. To be so easily contented, to accommodate one's self with such philosophy to one's circumstances,—what an advantage that is ! But it required no philosophy on the part of the girls, who had not imagination enough to think of anything different, and who devoutly believed that nothing on earth was so virtuous, so dignified, so praiseworthy, as to keep the linen in order, and make your own underclothing, and sit round the fire at home. When any one would read aloud to them they wanted no better paradise ; but they were not very exacting even in the matter of reading aloud. However exciting the book might be, they were quite willing that it should be put away at a quarter to ten, with a book-marker in it to keep the place. Once Chatty had been known to take it up clandestinely after prayers, to see whether the true murderer was found out; but Minnie waited quite decorously till eight o'clock next evening, which was the right hour for resuming the reading. Happy girls ! They thus had in their limited little world quite a happy life, expecting nothing, growing no older from year to year. Minnie was twenty-five, Chatty twenty-three : they were good-looking enough in their quiet way, very neat and tidy, with brown hair so well brushed that it reflected the light. Theodore was the youngest, and he had been very welcome when he came ; for otherwise the property would have gone to a distant heir of entail, which would not have been pleasant for any of the family. He had been a very quiet boy so long as he was at home, though not perhaps in the same manner of quietness as that of the girls ; but since he was thirteen he had been away for the greater part of the years, appearing only in the holidays, when he was always reading for something or other,—so that nobody was aware how great was the difference between the fastidious young scholar and the rest of his belongings.

Mr. Warrender himself was not a scholar. He had got through life very well without ever being at the university. In his day it was not considered such a necessity as now. And he was not at all critical of his son. So long as the boy got into no scrapes he asked no more of him. He was

quite complacent when Theo brought home his school prizes,
and used to point them out to visitors. "This is for his
Latin verses," he would say. "I don't know where the
boy got a turn for poetry. I am sure it was not from me."
The beautiful smooth binding and the school arms on the
side gave him great gratification. He had a faint notion
that as Theo brought home no prizes from Oxford he was
not perhaps getting on so well; but naturally he knew
nothing of his son's experiences with the Rector and the
dons. And by that time he was ill and feverish, and far
more taken up about his beef-tea than about anything else
in the world. They did not make it half strong enough.
If they only would make it strong he felt sure he would
soon regain his strength. But how could a man pick up,
who was allowed nothing but slops, when his beef-tea was
like water? This was the matter that occupied him most,
while his son was going through the ordeal above described,
—there never was any taste in the beef-tea. Mr. Warrender
thought the cook must make away with the meat; or else
send the best of the infusion to some of her people in the
village, and give it to him watered. When it was made
over the fire in his room he said his wife had no skill; she
let all the goodness evaporate. He never could be satisfied
with his beef-tea; and so, grumbling and indignant, finding
no savour in anything, but thoroughly convinced that this

was "their" fault, and that they could make it better if
they were to try, he dwindled and faded away.

It was a long illness; a family gets used to a long illness, and after a while accepts it as the natural course of
events.   And the doctor had assured them all that no
sudden "change" was to be looked for.   Nevertheless,
there was a sudden change.   It had become the routine of
the house that each of the ladies should spend so many
hours with papa.   Mrs. Warrender was with him, of course,
the greater part of the day, and went out and in to see if
he was comfortable every hour or two during the night;
but one of the girls always sat with him in the evening,
bringing her needlework upstairs, and feeling that she was
doing her duty in giving up the reading just when the book
was at its most interesting point.   It was after Chatty had
fulfilled this duty, and everybody was serenely preparing to
go to bed, that the change came.   "How is he?" Mrs.
Warrender had said, as they got out the Prayer-Book which
was used at family prayers.   "Just as usual, mamma : quite
quiet and comfortable.   I think he was asleep, for he took
no notice when I bade him good-night," Chatty said ; and
then the servants came in, and the little rites were accomplished.   Mrs. Warrender then went upstairs, and received
the same report from her maid, who sat with the patient
in the intervals when the ladies were at prayers.   "Quite

comfortable, ma'am, and I think he is asleep." Mrs. Warrender went to the bedside and drew back the curtain softly,—the red moreen curtain which was like a board suspended by the head of the bed,—and lo, while they all had been so calm, the change had come.

The girls thought their mother made a great deal more fuss than was necessary; for what could be done? It might be right to send for the doctor, who is an official whose presence is essential at the last act of life; but what was the good of sending a man on horseback into Highcombe, on the chance of the telegraph office being still open? Of course it was not open; and if it had been, Theo could not possibly leave Oxford till next morning. But then it was a well-known fact that mamma was excitable, and often did things without thought. He lingered all night, "just alive, and that is all," the doctor said. It was Chatty who sent for the rector, who came and read the prayers for the sick at the bedside, but agreed with Dr. Durant that it was of no use attempting to rouse the departing soul from the lethargy in which he lay. And before Theodore arrived all was over. He knew it before he entered the house by the sight of the drawn blinds, which received him with a blank whiteness of woe as soon as he caught sight of the windows. They had not sent to meet him at the station, thinking he would not come till the later train.

"Try and get mamma to lie down," Minnie said, as she kissed her brother. "She is going on exciting herself for nothing. I am sure everything was done that could be done, and we can do him no good by making ourselves more miserable now."

Minnie had cried in the early morning as much as was right and natural,—her eyes were still a little red; but she did not think it necessary to begin over again, as Chatty did, who had a tendency to overdo everything, like mamma. As for Theodore, he did not cry at all, but grew very pale, and did not say a word when he was taken into the chamber of death. The sight of that marble, or rather waxen, figure lying there had a greater effect upon his imagination than upon that of either of the girls, who perhaps had not got much imagination to be affected. He was overawed and silenced by that presence, which he had never met before so near. When his mother threw herself into his arms, with that excess of emotion which was peculiar to her, he held her close to him with a throb of answering feeling. The sensation of standing beside that which was not, although it was, his father, went through and through the being of the sensitive young man. Death is always most impressive in the case of a commonplace person, with whom we have no associations but the most ordinary ones of life. What had come to him?—to the mind which had been so

much occupied with the quality of his beef-tea? Was it
possible that he could have leaped all at once into the
contemplation of the highest subjects, or must there not be
something intermediate between the beef-tea and the *Gloria
in Excelsis?* This was the thought, inappropriate, unnatural,
as he felt it, which came into his mind as he stood by the
bed upon which lay that which had been the master of the
Warren yesterday, and now was " the body"; a solemn,
inanimate thing arranged with dreadful neatness, presently
to be taken away and hid out of sight of the living. Tears
did not come even when he took his mother into his arms,
but only a dumb awe not unmixed with horror, and even that
sense of repulsion with which some minds regard the dead.

It was the height of summer, the time at which the
Warren looked its best. The sunshine, which scarcely got
near it in the darker part of the year, now penetrated the
trees on every side, and rushed in as if for a wager, every
ray trying how far it could reach into the depths of the
shade. It poured full into the drawing-room by one window,
so that Minnie was mindful at all times to draw down that
blind, that the carpet might not be spoiled; and of course
all the blinds were down now. It touched the front of the
house in the afternoon, and blazed upon the lawn, making
all the flowers wink. Inside, to people who had come out
of the heat and scorching of other places more open to the

influences of the skies, the coolness of the Warren in June
was delightful. The windows stood open, the hum of bees
came in, the birds made an unceasing chorus in the trees.
Neither birds nor bees took the least notice of the fact that
there was death in the house. They carried on their jubila-
tion, their hum of business, their love-making and nursery
talk, all the same, and made the house sound not like a
house of mourning, but a house of rejoicing ; all this harmonious noise being doubly audible in the increased stillness of the place, where Minnie thought it right to speak in
a whisper, and Chatty was afraid to go beyond the example
of her sister. Mrs. Warrender kept her room, except in
the evening, when she would go out with Theo for a little
air. Only in the grounds ! no farther,—through the woods,
which the moonlight pierced with arrows of silver, as far as
the pond, which shone like a white mirror with all the great
leaves of the water-lilies black upon its surface. But the girls
thought that even this was too much. They could not think
how she could feel able for it before the funeral. They sat
with one shaded lamp and the shutters all closed, " reading
a book," which was their severest estimate of gravity. That
is to say, each had a book : one a volume of sermons, the
other *Paradise Lost*, which had always been considered
Sunday reading by the Warrenders, and came in very con-
veniently at this moment. They had been busy all day

with the maid and the dressmaker from the village, getting their mourning ready. There were serious doubts in their minds how high the crape ought to come on their skirts, and whether a cuff of that material would be enough without other trimmings on the sleeves; but as it was very trying to the eyes to work at black in candlelight, they had laid it all aside out of sight, and so far as was possible out of thought, and composed themselves to read as a suitable occupation for the evening, less cheerful than either coloured or white needlework, and more appropriate. It was very difficult, especially for Minnie, upon whom the chief responsibility would rest, to put that question of the crape out of her thoughts; but she read on in a very determined manner, and it is to be hoped that she succeeded. She felt very deeply the impropriety of her mother's proceedings. She had never herself stirred out-of-doors since her father's death, and would not till after the funeral, should the interests of nations hang on it. She, at least, knew what her duty was, and would do it. Chatty was not so sure on this subject, but she had been more used to follow Minnie than to follow mamma, and she was loyal to her traditions. One window was open a little behind the half-closed shutters, and let in something of the sounds and odours of the night. Chatty was aware that the moon was at the full, and would have liked to stretch her young limbs with a run; but she dared not even think of such a thing in sight of Minnie's face.

"I wonder how long mamma means to stay. One would think she was *enjoying* it," Minnie said, with a little emphasis on the word. As she used it, it seemed the most reprehensible verb in the world.

"She likes to be with Theo," said Chatty; "and she is always such a one for the air."

"Likes!" said her sister. "Is this a time to think of what one likes, with poor dear papa in his coffin?"

"She never left him as long as he wanted her," said the apologetic sister.

"No, indeed, I should hope not; that would have been criminal. Poor dear mamma would never do anything really bad; but she does not mind if she does a thing that is unusual. It is *very* unusual to go out before the funeral; it is a thing that is never done, especially by the ladies of the house."

"Shall we be able to go out on Friday, Minnie?" Friday was the funeral day.

"It would be very bad taste, I think. Of course, if it does not prove too much for us, we ought to go to church to meet the procession. Often it is thought to be too much for the ladies of a family."

"I am sure it would not be too much for me. Oh, I

shall go as far as we can go with him—to the grave, Minnie."

"You had better wait till you see whether it will not be too much for you," said the elder sister, while Chatty dried her eyes. Minnie's eyes had no need of drying. She had cried at the right time, but it was little more than levity to be always crying. It was nearly as bad as enjoying anything. She did not like extravagance of any kind.

And then they turned to their reading again, and felt that, whatever mamma might think herself at liberty to do, they, at least, were paying that respect to their father's memory which young women in a well-regulated household should always be the first to pay.

CHAPTER III.

MEANWHILE the mother and son took their walk. It was a very silent walk, without much outward trace of that enjoyment which Minnie had felt so cruelly out of place : but no doubt to both there was a certain pleasure in it. Mr. Warrender had now been lying in that silent state which the most insignificant person holds immediately after death, for three days, and there was still another to come before he could be laid away in the dark and noisome bed in the family vault, where all the Warrenders made their last assertion of superiority to common clay. This long and awful pause in the affairs of life was intolerable to the two people now walking softly through the paths of the little wood, where the moonbeams shone through the trees ; to the son, because he was of an impatient nature, and could not endure the artificial gloom which was thus forced upon him. He had felt keenly all those natural sensations which the loss of a father calls forth : the breaking of an old tie, the oldest in the world ; the breach of all the habits of his life ;

the absence of the familiar greeting, which had always been
kind enough, if never enthusiastic; the general overturn
and loss of the usual equilibrium in his little world. It was
no blame to Theo if his feelings went little further than this.
His father had been no active influence in his life. His
love had been passive, expressing itself in few words, without sympathy in any of the young man's pursuits, or know-
ledge of them, or desire to know,—a dull affection because
the boy belonged to him, and satisfaction in that he had
never got into any scrapes or given any trouble. And the
return which the son made was in the same kind. Theo
had felt the natural pang of disruption very warmly at the
moment; he had felt a great awe and wonder at sight of
the mystery of that pale and solemn thing which had lately
been so unmysterious and unsolemn. But even these pangs
of natural sensation had fallen into a little ache and weari-
ness of custom, and his fastidious soul grew tired of the
bonds that kept him, or would have kept him, precisely at
the same point of feeling for so many hours and days.
This is not possible for any one, above all for a being of
his temper, and he was restless beyond measure, and eager
to get over this enforced pause, and emerge into the common
life and daylight beyond. The drawn blinds somehow
created a stifling atmosphere in his very soul.

Mrs. Warrender felt it was indecorous to begin to speak

of plans and what was to be done afterwards, so long as her dead husband was still master of the oppressed and melancholy house; but her mind, as may be supposed, was occupied by them in the intervals of other thoughts. She was not of the Warrender breed, but a woman of lively feelings; and as soon as the partner of her life was out of her reach she had begun to torment herself with fears that she had not been so good to him as she ought. There was no truth, at least no fact, in this, for there could have been no better wife or more careful nurse. But yet, as every individual knows more of his or her self than all the rest of the world knows, Mrs. Warrender was aware that there were many things lacking in her conjugal devotion. She had not been the wife she knew how to be; in her heart she had never given herself credit for fulfilling her duty. Oh yes, she had fulfilled all her duties. She had been everything to him that he wanted, that he expected, that he was capable of understanding. But she knew very well that when all is said, that is not everything that can be said; and now that he was dead, and could no longer look in her face with lack-lustre eyes, wondering what the deuce the woman meant, she threw herself back upon her own standard, and knew that she had not come up to it. Even now she could not come up to it. Her heart ought to be desolate; life ought to hold nothing for her but perhaps resignation, perhaps despair. She ought to be beyond all feeling for what was to come. Yet she was not so. On the contrary, new ideas, new plans, had welled up into her mind,—how many, how few hours after she had laid down the charge, in which outwardly she had been so faithful, but inwardly so full of shortcomings? These plans filled her mind now as she went by her son's side through the mossy paths where, even in the height of summer, it was always a little cold. She could not speak of them, feeling a horror of herself, an ashamed sense that to betray the revulsion of her thoughts to her boy would be to put her down from her position in his respect for ever. Between these mutual reluctances to betray what was really in them the two went along very silently, as if they were counting their steps, their heads a little bowed down, the sound of their feet making far more commotion than was necessary in the stillness of the place. To be out-of-doors was something for both of them. They could breathe more freely, and if they could not talk could at least think, without the sense that they were impairing the natural homage of all things to the recently dead.

"Take care, Theo," she said, after a long interval of silence. "It is very damp here."

"Yes, there is a good deal of timber that ought to go." He caught his breath when he had said this, and she gave

a slight shiver. They both would have spoken quite freely
had the father been alive. " The house is damp, too," said
he, taking courage.

" In winter, perhaps, a little, when there is much
rain."

And then there was a long pause. When they came
within sight of the pond, which glistened under the moonlight, reflecting all the trees in irregular masses, and showing
here and there a big white water-lily bud couched upon a
dark bank of leaves, he spoke again : " I don't think it
can be very healthy, either, to have the pond so near the
house."

" You have always had your health, all of you," she
said.

" That is true ; but not very much of it. We are a
subdued sort of family, mother."

" That is because the Warrenders——" She stopped
here, feeling the inappropriateness of what she was about to
say. It very often happens that a wife has but little opinion
of the race to which her husband belongs. She attributes
the defects of her own children to that side instinctively.
" It is character," she said, " not health."

" But all the same, if we had a little more air and a
little less shade——"

He was becoming bolder as he went on.

"Theo," she said tremulously, "it is too soon to begin to talk of that."

And then there was a pause again. When they came to the edge of the pond, and stopped to look at the water-lilies, and at the white flood of the moonlight, and all the clustering masses of the trees that hung round as if to keep it hidden and sheltered, it was she who spoke : " Your father was very fond of this view. Almost the last time he was out we brought him here. He sat down for a long time, and was quite pleased. He cared for beautiful things much more than he ever said."

The thought that passed through Theo's mind was very rapid, that it might well be so, seeing nothing was ever said on the subject; but his remark was, "Very likely, mother," in a soft and soothing voice.

"I should be very sorry to see any—I mean I hope you will not make much alteration here."

"It is too soon," he said hastily, "to speak of that."

"Much too soon," she replied, with a quick sense of shame, taking her son's arm as they turned back. Even to turn back made the burden heavier, and dispelled the little advantage which they had got by the walk.

"There will be, I suppose, a great number of people —on Friday."

"Yes, I think a great number ; everybody about."

"What a nuisance! People might have sense enough
to know that at such a moment we don't want a lot of
strange faces peering at us, finding out how we bear up."

"My dear, it would have pleased him to know everybody would be there."

"I suppose so," said Theo, in a tone which was half
angry and half resigned.

"We will have to take a little thought how they are to
go. Lord Markland must come first, after the relations."

"Why? They never took much notice of us, and my
father never liked him. I don't see why he should come
at all."

"Oh yes, he will come, and your dear father would
have liked it. The Warrenders have always thought a
great deal of such things."

"I am a Warrender, I hope, and I don't."

"Ah, Theo, you! But you are much more like my
family," she said, with a little pressure of his arm.

This did not give him so much pleasure as it did her;
for, after all, however near a man may be to his mother's
family, he generally prefers his own, and the name which it
is his to bear. They got back under the thick shadow of
the trees when the conversation came to this point, and
once more it was impressed upon both that the path was
very damp, and that even in June it was difficult to get

through without wet feet; but Mrs. Warrender had felt herself checked by her son's reply about the alterations, and Theo felt that to betray how much he was thinking of them would be horrifying to his mother: so they both stepped into the marshy part without a word.

"You are still decided to go on Friday,—you and the girls?"

"Surely, Theo: we are all in good health, Heaven be praised! I should not feel that I had done everything if I did not go."

"You are sure it will not be too much for you, mother?"

This question went to her heart. She knew that it ought to be too much for her. Had she been the wife she ought to have been, the widow with a broken heart, then, perhaps, there might have been a doubt. But she knew also that it would not be too much for her. Her heart ached for the ideal anguish, which nobody looked for, nor would have understood. "He would have liked it," she said, in a subdued voice. That, at least, was quite true: and to carry out all his wishes thus faithfully was something, although she could not pay him the homage which was his due,—the supreme compliment of a broken heart.

At last Friday came. It was a dull day, of the colour most congenial to such a ceremony. A gentle shower fell

upon the wreaths and crosses that covered the coffin. There
was a large assembly from all the country round, for Mr.
Warrender had been a man who never harmed anybody,
which is perhaps a greater title to respect than those possess
who have taken more trouble. When you try to do good,
especially in a rural place, you are sure to stir up animo-
sities; but Mr. Warrender had never stirred up anybody.
He was greatly respected. Lord Markland was what the
farmers called "a wild young sprig," with little regard to
the proprieties; but he was there, and half the clergymen
of the diocese, and every country gentleman on the west
side of the county. The girls from behind their crape
veils watched the procession filing into church, and were
deeply gratified; and Mrs. Warrender felt that he would
have liked it, and that everything was being done according
to his wishes. She said to herself that this was what he
would have done for her if she had died first; and immediately there rose before her eyes (also behind her crape
veil) a picture of what might have been, had the coffin in
the middle of the church been hers; how he would have
stepped and looked, and the way in which he would have
held out his hand silently to each of the company, and the
secret pleasure in the fulfilment of all that was just and
right which would have been in his mind. It was instant-
aneous, it was involuntary, it made her smile against her

will; but the smile recalled her to herself, and overwhelmed
her with compunction and misery.   Smile—when it was he
who lay there in the coffin, under that black pall, expecting
from her the last observances, and that homage which
ought to come from a breaking heart !

The blinds were drawn up when they returned home,
the sunshine pouring in, the table spread.   Minnie, leading
Chatty with her, not without a slight struggle on that young
lady's part, retired to her room, and lay down a little, which
was the right thing to do.   She had a tray brought upstairs,
and was not disinclined for her luncheon : mercifully, their
presence at the funeral had not been too much for them.
And all the mourning was complete and everything in order,
even so far as to the jet necklaces which the girls put on
when they went down to tea.   Mrs. Warrender had been
quite overcome on re-entering the house, feeling, though
she had so suffered from the long interval before the funeral,
that to come back to a place from which he had now been
solemnly shut out for ever was more miserable than all that
had gone before ; for it will be perceived that she was not
of the steady mettle of the others, but a fantastic woman,
who changed her mind very often, and whose feelings were
always betraying her.   The funeral had been early, and the
distant visitors had been able to leave in good time, so that
there was no need for a large luncheon party ; and the

lawyer and a cousin of Mr. Warrender's were the only strangers who shared that meal with the mother and son. Then, as a proper period had now been arrived at, and as solicitors rush in where heirs fear to tread, open questions were asked about the plans of the family and what Theo meant to do. He said at once, " I see no need for plans. Why should there be any discussion of plans? So far as outward circumstances go, what change is there? My mother and the girls will just go on as usual, and I, of course, will go back to Oxford. It will be more than a year before I can take my degree."

He thought—but no doubt he must have been mistaken—that a blank look came over his mother's face; but it was so impossible that she could have thought of anything else that he dismissed the idea from his mind. She said nothing, but Mr. Longstaffe replied—

" At present that is no doubt the wisest way; but I think it is always well that people should understand each other at once and provide for all emergencies, so that there may be no wounded feeling, or that sort of thing, hereafter. You know, Mrs. Warrender, that the house in Highcombe has always been the jointure house?"

" Yes," she said, with a certain liveliness in her answer, almost eagerness. " My husband has often told me so."

" We are authorised to put it in perfect repair, and you

are authorised to choose whatever you please out of the furniture at the Warren to make it according to your taste. Perhaps we had better do that at once, and put it into your hands. If you don't live there, you can let it, or lend it, or make some use of it."

" It might be convenient," Mrs. Warrender said, with a slight hesitation, " if Theodore means, as I suppose he does, to carry out improvements here."

And yet she had implored him yesterday not to make many alterations ! Theo felt a touch of offence with his mother. He began to think there was something in the things the girls used to say, that you never knew when you had mamma, or whether she might not turn upon you in a moment. She grew much more energetic, all at once, and even her figure lost the slight stoop of languor that was in it. " If you are going to cut any trees, or do any drainage, Theo, we could all live there while the works went on."

He gave a slight start in person, and a much greater in spirit, and a fastidious curve came to his forehead. " I don't know that I shall cut any trees now. You know you said the other day, We can talk of that after."

" Oh yes, it is early days," said the lawyer. " Of course it is not as if there were other heirs coming in, or any compulsory division were to be made. You can take your time. But I have always observed that things went

smoother when it was understood from the first, in case of
a certain emergency arising, or new conditions of any kind,
so and so should follow.   You understand what I mean."

"It is always wisest," said the Warrender cousin, "to
have it all put down hard and fast, so that nobody may be
disappointed, whatever should happen.   Of course Theo
will marry."

"I hope so," said his mother, permitting herself to
smile.

"Of course he will marry," said the lawyer.

"But he had better take his degree first," the cousin
added, feeling that he had distinguished himself; "and in
the meantime the girls and you will have time to look
about you.   Highcombe is rather a dull place.   And then
the house is large.   You could not get on in it with less
than four or five servants."

"Four would do," said Mr. Longstaffe.

"And supposing my cousin kept a pony chaise, or
something?   She could not get on without a pony chaise.
That means another."

Theodore pushed back his chair from the table with
a harsh peremptoriness, startling them all.   "I am sure my
mother doesn't want to go into these calculations," he said;
"neither do I.   Leave us alone to settle what we find to
be best."

"Dear me," said cousin Warrender, " I hope you don't imagine me to have any wish to interfere." Theo did not make any reply, but gave his mother his arm, and led her upstairs.

" I did not wish you to be troubled with business at all ; certainly not to-day," he said to her, half apologetically. But there was something in her face which he did not quite understand, as she thanked him and smiled, with an inclination to cry. Was it possible that she was a little disappointed to have the discussion stopped, and that she took much interest in it, and contemplated not at all with displeasure the prospect of an entire change in her life ?

CHAPTER IV.

IT will be divined from what has been said that there was one element in the life at the Warren which has not yet been entered into, and that was Mrs. Warrender. The family were dull, respectable, and proper to their fingers' ends. But she was not dull. She had been Mr. Warrender's wife for six-and-twenty years,—the wife of a dull, good man, who never wanted any variety in his life, who needed no change, no outbursts of laughter or tears, nothing to carry away the superabundance of the waters of life. With him there had been no superabundance, there had never been any floods ; consequently there was no out-let necessary to carry them away. But she was a woman of another sort : she was born to hunger for variety, to want change, to desire everything that was sweet and pleasant. And lo ! fate bound her to the dullest life,—to marry Mr. Warrender, to live in the Warren. She had not felt it so much in the earlier part of her life, for then she had to some extent what her spirit craved. She had

children : and every such event in a woman's life is like
what going into battle is to a man,—a thing for which all
his spirits collect themselves, which she may come out of
or may not, an enormous risk, a great crisis. And when
the children were young, before they had as yet betrayed
themselves what manner of spirits they were, she had her
share of the laughter and the tears ; playing with her babies,
living for them, singing to them, filling her life with them,
and expecting as they grew up that all would be well.
Many women live upon this hope. They have not had
the completion of life in marriage which some have ; they
have failed in the great lottery, either by their own fault or
the fault of others : but the children, they say to themselves,
will make all right. The *désillusionment* which takes this
form is the most bitter of all. The woman who has not
found in her husband that dearest friend, whose companionship can alone make life happy, when she discovers
after a while that the children in whom she has placed her
last hope are his children, and not hers,—what is to become
of her? She is thrown back upon her own individuality
with a shock which is often more than flesh and blood can
bear. In Mrs. Warrender's case this was not, as in some
cases, a tragical discovery, but it had an exasperating and
oppressive character which was almost more terrible. She
had been able to breathe while they were children ; but

when they grew up they stifled her, each with the same "host of petty maxims" which had darkened the still air from her husband's lips. How, in face of the fact that she had been their teacher and guide far more than their father ever was, they should have learned these, and put aside everything that was like her or expressed her sentiments, was a mystery which she never could solve; but so it was. Mr. Warrender was what is called a very good father. He did not spoil them; bonbons of any kind, physical or spiritual, never came to them from his hands. He could not be troubled with them much as babies, but when they grew old enough to walk and ride with him he liked their company; and they resembled him, which is always flattering. But he had taken very little notice of them during the first twelve years or so of their life. During that time they had been entirely in their mother's hands, hearing her opinions, regulated outwardly by her will: and yet they grew up their father's children, and not hers! How strange it was, with a touch of the comic which made her laugh! —that laugh of exasperation and impatience which marks the intolerable almost more than tears do. How was it? Can any one explain this mystery? She was of a much more vivacious, robust, and vigorous race than he was, for the level of health among the Warrenders, like the level of being generally, was low; but this lively, warm-blooded,

energetic creature was swallowed up in the dull current of
the family life, and did not affect it at all. She nursed them,
ruled them, breathed her life into them, in vain : they were
their father's children,—they were Warrenders born.

This was not precisely the case with Theo, her only
son. To him she had transmitted something; not her
energy and love of life, but rather something of that exasperated impatience which was so often the temper of her
mind in later years, though suppressed by all the powers of
self-control she possessed, and modified, happily, by the
versatility of her nature, which could not brood and mope
over one subject, however deeply that might enter into her
life. This impatience took in him the form of a fastidious
intolerance, a disposition to start aside at a touch, to put
up with nothing, to hear no reason even, when he was
offended or crossed. He was like a restive horse, whom
the mere movement of a shadow, much more the touch of
a rein or the faintest vibration of a whip, sets off in the
wildest gallop of nervous self-will or self-assertion. The
horse, it is to be supposed, desires his own way as much
as the man does when he bolts or starts. Theo was in
this respect wonderfully unlike the strain of the Warrenders,
but he was not on that account more like his mother; and
he had so much of the calm of the paternal blood in his
veins along with this unmanageableness that he was as

contented as the rest with the quiet of the home life, and so long as he was permitted to shut himself up with his book wished for no distraction,—nay, disliked it, and thought society and amusements an intolerable bore.

Thus it was the mother alone to whom the thought of change was pleasant. A woman of forty-five in widow's weeds, who had just nursed her husband through a long illness and lost him, and whose life since she was nineteen had been spent in this quiet house among all these still surroundings, amid the unchangeable traditions of rural life,—who could have ventured to imagine the devouring impatience that was within her, the desire to flee, to shake the dust off her feet, to leave her home and all her associations, to get out into the world and breathe a larger air and be free? Sons and daughters may entertain such sentiments; even the girls, whose life, no doubt, had been a dull one, might be supposed willing enough, with a faint pretence of natural and traditionary reluctance, and those few natural tears which are wiped so soon, to leave home and see the world. But the mother! In ordinary circumstances it would have been the duty of the historian to set forth the hardness of Mrs. Warrender's case, deprived at once, by her husband's death, not only of her companion and protector, but of her home and position as head of an important house. Such a case is no doubt often a hard one. It adds a hundred little humiliations to grief, and makes bereavement downfall, the overthrow of a woman's importance in the world, and her exile from the sphere in which she has spent her life. We should be far more sure of the reader's sympathy if we pictured her visiting for the last time all the familiar haunts of past years, tearing herself away from the beloved rooms, feeling the world a blank before her as she turned away.

On the contrary, it is scarcely possible to describe the chill of disappointment in her mind when Theo put an abrupt stop to all speculations, and offered her his arm to lead her upstairs. She ought, perhaps, to have wanted his support to go upstairs, after all, as her maid said, that she had "gone through": but she did not feel the necessity. She would have preferred much to know what was going to be done, to talk over everything, to be able to express without further sense that they were premature and inappropriate, as much as it would be expedient to express of her own wishes. The absolute repression of those five dark days, during which she had said nothing, had been almost more intolerable to her than years of the repression which was past. When you know that nothing you can do or say is of any use, and that whatsoever struggle you may make will be wholly ineffectual to change your lot, it is comparatively easy, in the composure of impossibility, to

keep yourself down ; but when all at once you become again
master of your own fate, even a temporary curb becomes
intolerable. Mrs. Warrender went into her room by the
compulsion of her son and conventional propriety, and was
supposed to lie down on the sofa and rest for an hour or
two. Her maid arranged the cushions for her, threw a
shawl over her feet, and left her on tip-toe, shutting the
door with elaborate precautions. Mrs. Warrender remained
still for nearly half an hour. She wept, with a strange
mixture of feelings ; partly out of a poignant sense of the
fictitiousness of all these observances by which people were
supposed to show " respect " to the dead, and partly out
of a real aching of the heart and miserable sense that even
now, that certainly by and by, the man who had been so
all-important a little while ago would be as if he had not
been. She wept for him, and yet at the same time wept
because she could not weep more for him, because the
place which knew him had already begun to know him no
more, and because of the sham affliction with which they
were all supplementing the true. It was she who shed the
truest tears, but it was she also who rebelled most at the
make-believe which convention forced upon her ; and the
usual sense of hopeless exasperation was strong in her
mind. After a while she threw off the shawl from her
feet and the cushions that supported her shoulders, and

got up and walked about the room, looking out upon the
afternoon sunshine and the trees that were turning their
shadows to the east. How she longed, with a fervour
scarcely explainable, not at all comprehensible to most
people, to leave the place, to open her wings in a large
atmosphere, to get free!

At half-past four o'clock Minnie and Chatty went down
to tea. They were to the minute, and their mother heard
them with a half smile. It was always time enough for her
to smooth her hair and her collar, and take a new handker-
chief from her drawer, when she heard the sisters close
their door. She went downstairs after them, in her gown
covered with crape, with her snowy cap, which gave dignity
to her appearance. Her widow's dress was very becoming
to her, as it is to so many people. She had a pretty complexion, pure red and white, though the colour was perhaps
a little broken, and not so smooth as a girl's; and her eyes
were brown and bright. Notwithstanding the weeks of
watching she had gone through, the strain of everything
that had passed, she made little show of her trouble. Her
eye was not dim, nor her natural force abated. The girls
were dull in complexion and aspect, but their mother was
not so. As she came into the room there came with her a
brightness, a sense of living, which was inappropriate to
the hour and the place.

"Where is Theo?" she asked.

"He is coming in presently; at least, I called to him as he went out, and told him tea was ready, and he said he would be in presently," Chatty replied.

"I wish he would have stayed, if it had even been in the grounds, to-day," said Minnie. "It will look so strange to see him walking about as if nothing had happened."

"He has been very good; he has conformed to all our little rules," said the mother, with a sigh.

"Little rules, mamma? Don't you think it of import- ance, then, that every respect——"

"My dear," said Mrs. Warrender, "I am tired of hear- ing of every respect. Theo was always respectful and affectionate. I would not misconstrue him even if it should prove that he has taken a walk."

"On the day of dear papa's funeral!" cried Minnie, with a voice unmoved.

Mrs. Warrender turned away without any reply; partly because the tears sprang into her eyes at the matter-of-fact statement, and partly because her patience was exhausted.

"Have you settled, mamma, what he is going to do?" said Chatty.

"It is not for me to decide. He is twenty-one; he is his own master. You have not," Mrs. Warrender said, "taken time to think yet of the change in our circumstances.

Theo is now master here. Everything is his to do as he pleases."

"Everything!" said the girls in chorus, opening their eyes.

"I mean, of course, everything but what is yours and what is mine. You know your father's will. He has been very just, very kind, as he always was." She paused a little, and then went on : "But your brother, as you know, is now the master here. We must understand what his wishes are before we can settle on anything."

"Why shouldn't we go on as we always have done?" said Minnie. "Theo is too young to marry; besides, it would not be decent for a time, even if he wanted to, which I am sure he does not. I don't see why he should make any change. There is nowhere we can be so well as at home."

"Oh, nowhere!" said Chatty.

Their mother sat and looked at them, with a dull throb in her heart. They had sentiment and right on their side, and nature too. Everybody would agree that for a bereaved family there was no place so good as home,—the house in which they were born and where they had lived all their life. She looked at them blankly, feeling how unnatural, how almost wicked, was the longing in her own mind to get away, to escape into some place where she could take

large breaths and feel a wide sky over her. But how was
she to say it, how even to conclude what she had been
saying, feeling how inharmonious it was with everything
around?

"Still," she said meekly, "I am of Mr. Longstaffe's
opinion that everything should be fully understood between
us from the first. If we all went on just the same, it migh
be very painful to Theo, when the time came for him to
marry (not now; of course there is no question of that
now), to feel that he could not do so without turning his
mother and sisters out-of-doors."

"Why should he marry, so long as he has us? It is
not as if he had nobody, and wanted some one to make
him a home. What would he do with the house if we were
to leave it? Would he let it? I don't believe he could
let it. It would set everybody talking. Why should he
turn his mother and sisters out-of-doors? Oh, I never
thought of anything so dreadful!" cried Minnie and Chatty,
one uttering one exclamation, and another the other. They
were very literal, and in the minds of both the grievance
was at once taken for granted. "Oh, I never could have
thought such a thing of Theo,—our own brother, and
younger than we are!"

The mother had made two or three ineffectual attempts
to stem the tide of indignation. "Theo is thinking of

nothing of the kind," she said at last, when they were out of breath. "I only say that he must not feel he has but that alternative when the time comes, when he may wish—when it may be expedient——No, no, he has never thought of such a thing. I only say it for the sake of the future, to forestall after-complications."

"Oh, I wish you wouldn't frighten one, mamma! I thought you had heard about some girl he had picked up at Oxford, or something. I thought we should have to turn out, to leave the Warren—which would break my heart."

"And mine too,—and mine too!" cried Chatty.

"Where we have always been so happy, with nothing to disturb us!"

"Oh, so happy! always the same, one day after another! It will be different," said the younger sister, crying a little, "now that dear papa—— But still no place ever can be like home."

And there was the guilty woman sitting by, listening to everything they said; feeling how good, how natural, it was, —and still more natural, still more seemly, for her, at her age, than for them at theirs,—yet conscious that this house was a prison to her, and that of all things in the world that which she wanted most was to be turned out and driven away!

"My dears," she said, not daring to betray this feeling,

"if I have frightened you, I did not mean to do it. The house in Highcombe, you know, is mine. It will be our home if—if anything should happen. I thought it might be wise to have that ready, to make it our headquarters, in case—in case Theo should carry out the improvements."

"Improvements!" they cried with one voice. "What improvements? How could the Warren be improved?"

"You must not speak to me in such a tone. There has always been a question of cutting down some of the trees."

"But papa would never agree to it ; papa said he would never consent to it."

"I think," said Mrs. Warrender, with a guilty blush, "that he—had begun to change his mind."

"Only when he was growing weak, then,—only when you over-persuaded him."

"Minnie! I see that your brother was right, and that this is not a time for any discussion," Mrs. Warrender said.

There was again a silence : and they all came back to the original state of mind from which they started, and remembered that quiet and subdued tones and an incapacity for the consideration of secular subjects were the proper mental attitude for all that remained of this day.

It was not, however, long that this becoming condition lasted. Sounds were heard as of voices in the distance, and then some one running at full speed across the gravel drive in front of the door, and through the hall. Minnie had risen up in horror to stop this interruption, when the door burst open, and Theo, pale and excited, rushed in. "Mother," he cried, "there has been a dreadful accident. Markland has been thrown by those wild brutes of his, and I don't know what has happened to him. It was just at the gates, and they are bringing him here. There is no help for it. Where can they take him to?"

Mrs. Warrender rose to her feet at once; her heart rising too almost with pleasure to the thrill of a new event. She hurried out to open the door of a large vacant room on the ground floor. "What was Lord Markland doing here?" she said. "He ought to have reached home long ago."

"He has been in *that* house in the village, mother. They seemed to think everybody would understand. I don't know what he has to do there."

"He has nothing to do there. Oh, Theo, that poor young wife of his! And had he the heart to go from— from—us, in our trouble—there!"

"He seems to have paid for it, whatever was wrong in it. Go back to the drawing-room, for here they are coming."

"Theo, they are carrying him as if he were——"

"Go back to the drawing-room, mother. Whatever it is, it cannot be helped," Theodore said. He did not

mean it, but there was something in his tone which re-
minded everybody—the servants, who naturally came rushing to see what was the matter, and Mrs. Warrender, who
withdrew at his bidding—that he was now the master of
the house.

CHAPTER V.

MARKLAND was a much more important place than the Warren. It was one of the chief places in the county in which the family had for many generations held so great a position. It was a large building, with all that irregularity of architecture which is dear to the English mind,—a record of the generations which had passed through it and added to it, in itself a noble historical monument, full of indications of the past. But it lost much of its effect upon the mind from the fact that it was in much less good order than is usual with houses of similar pretensions ; and above all because the wood around it had been wantonly and wastefully cut, and it stood almost unsheltered upon its little eminence, with only a few seedling trees, weedy and long, like boys who had outgrown their strength, straggling about the heights. The house itself was thus left bare to all the winds. An old cedar, very large but very feeble, in the tottering condition of old age to which some trees, like men, come, with two or three of its longest branches torn off by storm and decay, interposed its dark foliage over the lower roof of the west wing, and gave a little appearance of shelter, and a few Lombardy poplars and light-leaved young birches made a thin and interrupted screen to the east; but the house stood clear of these light and frivolous young attendants in a nakedness which made the spectator shiver.   The wood in the long avenue had been thinned in almost the same ruthless way, but here and there were shady corners, where old trees, not worth much in the market, but very valuable to the landscape, laid their heads together like ancient retainers, and rustled and nodded their disapproval of the devastation around.

Young Lady Markland, with her boy, on the afternoon of the June day on which Mr. Warrender was buried, walked up and down for some time in front of the house, casting many anxious looks down the avenue, by which, in its present denuded state, every approaching visitor was so easily visible.   She was still very young, though her child was about eight ; she having been married, so to speak, out of the nursery, a young creature of sixteen, a motherless girl, with no one to investigate too closely into the character of the young lover, who was not much more than a boy himself, and between whom and his girlish bride a hot, foolish young love had sprung up like a mushroom, in a week or two of acquaintance.   She was twenty-five, but did not look her age. She was small in stature,—one of those exquisitely neat little women whose perfection of costume and appearance no external accident disturbs. Her dress had the look of being moulded on her light little figure ; her hair was like brown satin, smooth as a mirror and reflecting the light. She did not possess the large grace of abstract beauty. There was nothing statuesque, nothing majestic, about her, but a kind of mild perfection, a fitness and harmony which called forth the approval of the more serious-minded portion of humanity as well as the admiration of the younger and more frivolous.

It was generally known in the county that this young lady had far from a happy life. She had been married in haste and over-confidence by guardians who, if not glad to be rid of her, were at least pleased to feel that their responsibility was over, and the orphan safe in her husband's care, without taking too much pains to prove that the husband was worthy of that charge, or that there was much reasonable prospect of his devotion to it. Young Markland, it was understood, had sown his wild oats somewhat plentifully at Oxford and elsewhere ; and it was therefore supposed, with very little logic, that there were no more to sow. But this had not proved to be the case, and almost before his young wife had reached the age of understanding, and was able to put two and two together, he had run through the fortune she brought him—not a very large one—and made her heart ache, which was worse, as hearts under twenty ought never to learn how to ache. She was not a happy wife. The country all about, the servants, and every villager near knew it, but not from Lady Markland. She was very loyal, which is a noble quality, and very proud, which in some cases does duty as a noble quality, and is accepted as such. What were the secrets of her married life no one ever heard from her; and fortunately those griefs which were open to all the world never reached her, at least in detail. She did not know, save vaguely, in what society her husband spent the frequent absences which separated him from her. She did not know what kind of friends he made, what houses he frequented, even in his own neighbourhood; and she was still under the impression that many of her wrongs were known by herself alone, and that his character had suffered but little in the eyes of the world.

There was one person, however, from whom she had not been able to hide these wrongs, and that was her child, —her only child. There had been two other babies, dead at their birth or immediately after, but Geoff was the only one who had lived, her constant companion, counsellor, and aid. At eight years old! Those who had never known what a child can be at that age, when thus entrusted with the perilous deposit of the family secrets, and elevated to the post which

his father ought but did not care to fill, were apt to think little
Geoff's development unnatural; and others thought, with
reason, that it was bad for the little fellow to be so constantly
with his mother, and it was said among the Markland relations that as he was now growing a great boy he ought to be
sent to school.   Poor little Geoff!   He was not a great boy,
nor ever would be.   He was small, *chétif,* unbeautiful; a little
sandy-haired, sandy-complexioned, insignificant boy, with no
features to speak of and no stamina, short for his age and of
uncertain health, which had indeed been the first reason of
that constant association with his mother which was supposed
to be so bad for him.   During the first years of his life,
which had been broken by continual illness, it was only
her perpetual care that kept him alive at all.   She had
never left him, never given up the charge of him to any
one; watched him by night and lived with him by day.
His careless father would sometimes say, in one of those
brags which show a heart of shame even in the breast of
the vicious, that if he had not left her so much to herself,
if he had dragged her about into society, as so many men
did their wives, she never would have kept her boy; and
perhaps there was some truth in it.   While he pursued his
pleasures in regions where no wife could accompany him,
she was free to devote all her life, and to find out every
new expedient that skill or science had thought of to

lengthen out the child's feeble days, and to gain time to
make a cure possible. He would never be very strong was
the verdict now, but with care he would live : and it was
she who had over again breathed life into him. This made
the tie a double one ; not out of gratitude, for the child
knew of no such secondary sentiment, but out of the
redoubled love which their constant association called forth.
They did not talk together of any family sorrows. It was
never intimated between them that anything wrong happened when papa was late and mamma anxious, or when
there were people at Markland who were not *nice*,—oh,
not a word ; but the child was anxious as well as mamma.
He too got the habit of watching, listening for the hurried
step, the wild rattle of the phaeton with those two wild
horses, which Lord Markland insisted on driving, up the
avenue. He knew everything, partly by observation, partly
by instinct. He walked with his mother now, clinging
with both hands to her arm, his head nearly on a level with
her shoulder, and close, close to it, almost touching, his
little person confused in the outline of her dress. The
sunshine lay full along the line of the avenue, just broken
in two or three places by the shadow of those old and
useless trees, but without a speck upon it or a sound.

"I don't think papa can be coming, Geoff, and it is
time you had your tea."

" Never mind me. I'll go and take it by myself, if you want me to, and you can wait here."

" Why?" she said. " It will not bring him home a moment sooner, as you and I know."

" No, but it feels as if it made him come; and you can see as far as the gate. It takes a long time to drive up the avenue. Oh yes, stop here; you will like that best."

" I am so silly," she said, which was her constant excuse. " When you are grown up, Geoff, I shall always be watching for you."

" That you shan't," said the boy. " I'll never leave you. You have had enough of that."

" Oh yes, my darling, you will leave me. I shall want you to leave me. A boy cannot be always with his mother. Come, now, I am going to be strong-minded. Let us go in. I am a little tired, I think."

" Perhaps the funeral was later than he thought," said the boy.

" Perhaps. It was very kind of papa to go. He does not like things of that kind; and he was not over-fond of Mr. Warrender, who, though he was very good, was a little dull. Papa doesn't like dull people."

" No. Do you like Theo Warrender, mamma?"

" Well enough," said Lady Markland. " I don't know him very much."

"I like him," said the child. "He knows a lot: he told me how to do that Latin. He is the sort of man I should like for my tutor."

"But he is a gentleman, Geoff. I mean, he would never be a tutor. He is as well off as we are,—perhaps better."

"Are men tutors only when they are not well off?"

"Well, dear, generally when they require the money. You could not expect young Mr. Warrender to come here and take a great deal of trouble, merely for the pleasure of teaching you."

"Why not?" said Geoff. "Isn't it a fine thing to teach children? It was you that said so, mamma."

"For me, dear, that am your mother; but not for a gentleman who is not even a relation."

"Gentlemen, to be sure, are different," said Geoff, with an air of deliberation. "There's papa, for in-stance——"

His mother threw up her hand suddenly. "Hark, Geoff! Do you hear anything?"

They had come indoors while this talk was going on, and were now seated in a large but rather shabby sitting-room, which was full of Geoff's toys and books. The windows were wide open, but the sounds from without came in subdued; for this room was at the back of the house, and at some distance from the avenue. They were both silent for some moments, listening, and then Lady Markland said, with an air of relief, " Papa is coming. I hear the sound of the phaeton."

" That is not the phaeton, mamma; that is only one horse," said Geoff, whose senses were very keen. When Lady Markland had listened a little longer, she acquiesced in this opinion.

" It will be some one coming to call," she said, with an air of resignation; and then they went on with their talk.

" Gentlemen are different; they don't take the charge of the children like you. However, in books," said Geoff, " the fathers very often are a great deal of good; they tell you all sorts of things. But books are not very like real life; do you think they are? Even Frank, in Miss Edgeworth, though you say he is so good, doesn't do things like me. I mean, I should never think of doing things like him; and no little girl would ever be so silly. Now, mamma, say true, what do you think? Would any little girl ever be so silly as to want the big bottle out of a physic shop? Girls may be silly, but not so bad as that."

" Perhaps, let us hope, she didn't know so much about physic shops, as you call them, as you do, my poor boy. I wonder who can be calling to-day, Geoff! I should have

thought that everybody near would be thinking of the
Warrenders, and—— It is coming very fast, don't you
think? But it does not sound like the phaeton."

"Oh no, it is not the phaeton. I'll go and look," said
Geoff. He came back in a moment, crying, " I told you
—it's a brougham ! Coming at such a pace !"

" I wonder who it can be !" Lady Markland said.

And when the boy resumed his talk she listened with
inattention, trying in vain to keep her interest fixed on what
he was saying, making vague replies, turning over a hundred
possibilities in her mind, but by some strange dulness, such
as is usual enough in similar circumstances, never thinking
of the real cause. What danger could there be to Markland in a drive of half a dozen miles, in the daylight; what
risk in Mr. Warrender's funeral? The sense that something
which was not an ordinary visit was coming grew stronger
and stronger upon her, but of the news which was about
to reach her she never thought at all.

At last the door opened. She rose hastily, unable to
control herself, to meet it, whatever it was. It was not a
ceremonious servant announcing a visit, but Theo Warrender, pale as death itself, with a whole tragic volume in
his face, but speechless, not knowing, now that he stood
before her, what to say, who appeared in the doorway.
He had hurried off, bringing his mother's little brougham

to carry the young wife to her husband's bedside; but it was not until he looked into her face and heard the low cry that burst from her that he realised what he had to tell. He had forgotten that a man requires all his skill and no small preparation to enable him to tell a young woman that her husband, who left her in perfect health a few hours before, was now on the brink of death. He stopped short on the threshold, awed by this thought, and only stared at her, not knowing what to say.

"Mr. Warrender!" she said, with the utmost surprise; then, with growing wonder and alarm, "You have come—— Something has happened!"

"Lady Markland—yes, there has been an accident. My mother—sent me with the brougham. I came off at once. Will you go back with me? The horse is very fast, and you can be there in half an hour."

This was all he could find to say. She went up to him, holding out her hands in an almost speechless appeal. "Why for me? Why for me? What has it got to do with me?"

He did not know how to answer her question. "Lady Markland!" he cried, "your husband——" and said no more.

She was at the door of the brougham in a moment. She had not taken off her garden hat, and she wanted no preparation. The child sprang to her side, caught her arm, and went with her without a word or question, as if that were undeniably his place. Everybody knew and remarked upon the singular union between the neglected young wife and her only child, but Warrender felt, he could scarcely tell why, that it annoyed and irritated him at this moment. When he put her into the carriage, and the boy clambered after her, he was unaccountably vexed by it,—so much vexed that his profound sympathy for the poor lady seemed somehow checked. Instead of following them into the carriage, which was not a very roomy one, he shut the door upon them sharply. " I will walk," he said. " I am not needed. Right, Jarvis, as fast as you can go." He stood by to see them dash off, Lady Markland giving him a surprised yet half-relieved look, in the paleness of her anxiety and misery. Then it suddenly became apparent to him that he had done what was best and most delicate, though without meaning it, out of the sudden annoyance which had risen within him. It was the best thing he could have done : but to walk six miles at the end of a fatiguing and trying day was not agreeable, and the sense of irritation was strong in him. " If ever I have anything to do with that boy——" he said involuntarily within himself. But what could he ever have to do with the boy, who probably by this time, little puny thing that he was, was Lord Markland, and the owner of all this great, bare, unhappy-looking place, eaten up by the locusts of waste and ruin.

The butler, an old servant, had been anxiously trying all this time to catch his eye. He came up now, as Warrender turned to follow on foot the carriage, which was already almost out of sight. "I beg your pardon, sir," he said, with the servant's usual formula, "but I've sent round for the dogcart, if you'll be so kind as to wait a few minutes. None of us, sir, but feels your kindness, coming yourself for my lady, and leaving her alone in her trouble, poor dear. Mr. Warrender, sir, if I may make so bold, what is the fact about my lord? Yes, sir, I heard what you told my lady; but I thought you would nat'rally say the best, not to frighten her. Is there any hope?"

"Not much, I fear. He was thrown out violently, and struck against a tree; they are afraid that his spine is injured."

"Oh, sir, so young! and oh, so careless! God help us, Mr. Warrender, we never know a step before us, do we, sir? If it's the spine, it will be no pain; and him so joky, more than his usual, going off them very steps this morning, though he was going to a funeral. Oh, Mr. Warrender, that I should speak so light, forgetting—— God bless us, what an awful thing, sir, after what has happened already, to happen in your house!"

Warrender answered with a nod,—he had no heart to speak ; and, refusing the dogcart, he set out on his walk home. An exquisite summer night : everything harsh stilled out of the atmosphere ; the sounds of labour ceasing ; a calm as of profoundest peace stealing over everything. The soft and subdued pain of his natural grief, hushed by that fatigue and exhaustion of both body and mind which a long strain produces, was not out of accord with the calm of nature. But very different was the harsh note of the new calamity, which had struck not the house in which the tragedy was being enacted, but this one, which lay bare and naked in the last light of the sinking sun. So young and so careless ! So young, so wasteful of life and all that life had to give, and now parted from it, taken from it at a blow !

CHAPTER VI.

LORD MARKLAND died at the Warren that night. He never recovered consciousness, nor knew that his wife was by his side through all the dreadful darkening of the summer evening, which seemed to image forth in every new tone of gathering gloom the going out of life. They told her as much as was necessary of the circumstances,—how, the distance between the Warren and the churchyard being so short, and the whole cortége on foot, Lord Markland's carriage had been left in the village; how he had stayed there to luncheon (presumably with the rector, for no particulars were given, nor did the bewildered young woman ask for any), which was the reason of his delay. The rest was very easily explained: everybody had said to him that "some accident" would happen one day or other with the horses he insisted on driving, and the prophecy had been fulfilled. Such prophecies are always fulfilled. Lady Markland was very quiet, accepting that extraordinary revolution in her life with a look of marble, and words that betrayed nothing.

Was she broken-hearted? was she only stunned by the suddenness, the awe, of such a catastrophe? The boy clung to her, yet without a tear, pale and silent, but never, even when the words were said that all was over, breaking forth into any childish outburst. He sat on the floor in her shadow, even when she was watching by the deathbed, never left her, keeping always a hold upon her arm, her hand, or her dress. Mrs. Warrender would have taken him away, and put him to bed,—it was so bad for him ; but the boy opposed a steady resistance, and Lady Markland put down her hand to him, not seeing how wrong it was to indulge him, all the ladies said. After this, of course nothing could be done, and he remained with her through all that followed. What followed was strange enough to have afforded a scene for a tragedy. Lady Markland asked to speak to Warrender, who had retired, leaving his mother, as was natural, to manage everything. He came to her at the door of the room which had so suddenly, with its bare, unused look, in the darkness of a few flickering candles, become a sort of presence chamber filled with the solemnity of dying. Her little figure, so neat and orderly, an embodiment of the settled peace and calm of life having nothing to do with tragedies, with the child close pressed against her side, his pale face looking as hers did, pale too and stony—never altogether passed from the memory of the man who came, reluctant, almost afraid, to hear what she had to say to him. It was like a picture against the darkness of the room,—a darkness both physical and moral, which centred in the curtained gloom behind, about which two shadowy figures were busy. Often and with very different sentiments he saw this group again, but never wholly forgot it, or had it effaced from the depths of his memory.

"Mr. Warrender," she said, in a voice which was very low, yet he thought might have been heard all over the house, "I want you to help me."

"Whatever I can do," he began, with some fervour, for he was young, and his heart was touched.

"I want," she continued, "to carry him home at once. I know it will not be easy, but it is night, and all is quiet. You are a man; you will know better how it can be done. Manage it for me."

Warrender was entirely unprepared for such a commission. "There will be great difficulties, dear Lady Markland," he said. "It is a long way. I am sure my mother would not wish you to think of her. This is a house of death. Let him stay."

She gave him a sort of smile, a softening of her stony face, and put out her hand to him. "Do it for me," she said. She was not at all moved by his objections,—perhaps she did not even hear them; but when she had thus repeated her command, as a queen might have done, she turned back into the room, and sat down, to wait, it seemed, until that command should be accomplished. Warrender went away with a most perplexed and troubled mind. He was half pleased, underneath all, that she should have sent for him and charged him with this office, but bewildered with the extraordinary commission, and not knowing what to do.

"What is it, Theo? What did she want with you?" his sisters cried, in subdued voices, but eager to know everything about Lady Markland, who had been as the stars in the sky to them a little while before.

He told them in a few words, and they filled the air with whispered exclamations. "How odd, how strange; oh, how unusual, Theo! People will say it is our doing. They will say, How dreadful of the Warrenders! Oh, tell her you can't do it! How could you do it, in the middle of the night!"

"That is just what I don't know," Warrender rejoined.

"Mr. Theo," said the old man, who was not dignified with the name of butler, "the lady is quite right. I can't tell you how it's to be done, but gardener, he is a very handy man, and he will know. The middle of the night—that's just what makes it easy, young ladies; and instead o' watching and waiting, the 'holl of us 'ull get to bed."

"That is all you're thinking of, Joseph."

"Well, it's a deal, sir, after all that's been going on in this house," Joseph said, with an aggrieved air. He had to provide supper, which was a thing unknown at the Warren, after all the trouble that every one had been put to. He was himself of opinion that to be kept up beyond your usual hours, and subjected to unexpected fatigues, made a "bit of supper" needful even for the uncomfortable and incomprehensible people whom he called the quality. They were a poorish lot, and he had a mild contempt for them, and to get them supper was a hardship; still, it was his own suggestion, and he was bound to carry it out.

It is unnecessary to enter into all Warrender's perplexities and all the expedients that were suggested. At last the handy gardener and himself hit upon a plan by which Lady Markland's wishes could be carried out. She sat still in the gloomy room where her husband lay dead, waiting till they should be ready; doubting nothing, as little disturbed by any difficulty as if it had been the simplest commission in the world which she had given the young man. Geoff sat at her feet, leaning against her, holding her hand. It is to be supposed that he slept now and then, as the slow moments went on, but whenever any one spoke to his mother his eyes would be seen gleaming against the darkness of her dress. They sat there waiting, perfectly still, with the candles flickering faintly about the room in the night air that breathed in through the open windows. The dark curtains had been drawn round the bed. It was like a catafalque looming darkly behind. Mrs. Warrender had used every persuasion to induce her guest to come into another room, to take something, to rest, to remember all that remained for her to do, and not waste her strength,—all those formulas which come naturally to the lips at such a moment. Lady Markland only answered with that movement of her face which was intended for a smile and a shake of her head.

At last the preparations were all complete. The night was even more exquisite than the evening had been; it was more still, every sound having died out of the earth except those which make up silence,—the rustling among the branches, the whirr of unseen insects, the falling of a leaf or a twig. The moon threw an unbroken light over the broad fields; the sky spread out all its stars, in myriads and myriads, faintly radiant, softened by the larger light; the air breathed a delicate, scarcely perceptible fragrance of growing grass, moist earth, and falling dew. How sweet, how calm, how full of natural happiness! Through this soft atmosphere and ethereal radiance a carriage made its way that was improvised with all the reverence and tenderness possible, in which lay the young man, dead, cut off in the

very blossom and glory of his days, followed by another in
which sat the young woman who had been his wife. What
she was thinking of who could tell? Of their half-childish
love and wooing, of the awaking of her own young soul to
trouble and disappointment, of her many dreary days and
years; or of the sudden severance, without a moment's
warning, without a leave-taking, a word, or a look? Perhaps all these things, now for a moment distinct, now
mingling confusedly together, formed the current of her
thoughts. The child, clasped in her arms, slept upon her
shoulder; nature being too strong at last for that which
was beyond nature, the identification of his childish soul
with that of his mother. She was glad that he slept, and
glad to be silent, alone, the soft air blowing in her face,
the darkness encircling her like a veil.

Warrender went with this melancholy cortége, making
its way slowly across the sleeping country. He saw everything done that could be done : the dead man laid on his
own bed; the living woman, in whom he felt so much
more interest, returned to the shelter of her home and
the tendance of her own servants. His part in the whole
matter was over when he stepped back into the brougham
which she had left. The Warrenders had seen but little of
the Marklands, though they were so near. The habits of
the young lord had naturally been little approved by Theo

Warrender's careful parents; and his manners, when the young intellectualist from Oxford met him, were revolting at once to his good taste and good breeding. On the other hand, the Warrenders were but small people in comparison, and any intimacy with Lord and Lady Markland was almost impossible. It was considered by all the neighbours "a great compliment" when Lord Markland came to the funeral. Ah, poor Markland, had he not come to the funeral! Yet how vain to say so, for his fate had been long prophesied, and what did it matter in what special circumstances it came to pass! But Warrender felt, as he left the house, that there could be no longer distance and partial acquaintance between the two families. Their lines of life—or was it of death?—had crossed and been woven together. He felt a faint thrill go through him,—a thrill of consciousness, of anticipation, he could not tell what. Certainly it was not possible that the old blank of non-connection could ever exist again. *She*, to whom he had scarcely spoken before, who had been so entirely out of his sphere, had now come into it so strangely, so closely, that she could never be separated from his thoughts. She might break violently the visionary tie between them,—she might break it, angry to have been drawn into so close a relation to any strangers,—but it never could be shaken off.

He drove quickly down the long bare avenue, where

all was so naked and clear, and put his head out of the
carriage window to look back at the house, standing out
bare and defenceless in the full moonlight, showing faintly,
through the white glory which blazed all around, a little
pitiful glimmer of human lights in the closed windows, the
watch-lights of the dead. It seemed a long time to the
young man since in his own house these watch-lights had
been extinguished. The previous event seemed to have
become dim to him, though he was so much more closely
connected with it, in the presence of this, which was more
awful, more terrible. He tried to return to the thoughts
of the morning, when his father was naturally in all things
his first occupation, but it was impossible to do it. Instead
of the thoughts which became him, as being now in his
father's place, with the fortunes and comfort of his family
more or less depending upon him, all that his mind would
follow were the events of this afternoon, so full of fate. He
saw Lady Markland stand, with the child clinging to her, in
the dim room, the shrouded bed and indistinct attendant
figures behind, the dimly flickering lights. Why had she
so claimed his aid, asked for his service, with that certainty
of being obeyed? Her every word trembled in his ear still :
—they were very few ; but they seemed to be laid up there
in some hidden repository, and came out and said themselves over again when he willed, moving him as he never

had been moved before. He made many efforts to throw off this involuntary preoccupation as the carriage rolled quickly along; the tired horse quickening its pace as it felt the attraction of home, the tired coachman letting it go almost at its own pleasure, the broad moonlight fields, with their dark fringes of hedge, spinning past. Then the village went past him, with all its sleeping houses, the church standing up like a protecting shadow. He looked out again at this, straining his eyes to see the dark spot where his father was lying, the first night in the bosom of the earth : and this thought brought him back for a moment to himself. But the next, as the carriage glided on into the shadow of the trees, and the overgrown copses of the Warren received him into their shadow, this other intrusive tragedy, this story which was not his, returned and took possession of him once more. To see her standing there, speaking so calmly, with the soft tones that perhaps would have been imperious in other circumstances : " Do it for me." No question whether it could be done, or if he could do it. One thing only there was that jarred throughout all,—the child that was always there, forming part of her. " If ever I have anything to do with that boy "— Warrender said to himself; and then there was a moment of dazzle and giddiness, and the carriage stopped, and a door opened, and he found himself standing out in the fresh, soft night with his mother, on the threshold of his own home. There was a light in the hall behind her, where she stood, with the whiteness of the widow's cap, which was still a novelty and strange feature in her, waiting till he should return. It was far on in the night, and except herself the household was asleep. She came out to him, wistfully looking in his face by the light of the moon.

"You did everything for her, Theo?"

"All that I could. I saw him laid upon his bed. There was nothing more for me to do."

"Are you very tired, my boy? You have done so much."

"Not tired at all. Come out with me a little. I can't go in yet. It is a lovely night."

"Oh, Theo, lovely and full of light!—the trees, and the bushes, and every blade of grass sheltering something that is living; and yet death, death reigning in the midst."

She leaned her head upon his arm and cried a little, but he did not make any response. It was true, no doubt, but other thoughts were in his mind.

"She will have great trouble with that child, when he grows up," he said, as if he had been carrying on some previous argument. "It is ridiculous to have him always hanging about her, as if he could understand."

Mrs. Warrender started, and the movement made his

arm which she held tremble, but he did not think what this
meant. He thought she was tired, and this recalled his
thoughts momentarily to her. "Poor mother!" he said;
"you sat up for me, not thinking of your own fatigue and
trouble, and you are over-tired. Am I a trouble to you,
too ?" His mind was still occupied with the other train of
thinking, even when he turned to subjects more his own.

"Do you know," she said, not caring to reply, "it is
the middle of the night?"

"Yes, and you should be in bed. But I couldn't sleep.
I have never had anything of the kind to do before, and it
takes all desire to rest out of one. It will soon be daylight.
I think I shall take my bath, and then get to work."

"Oh no, Theo. You would not work,—you would
think; and there are some circumstances in which thinking
is not desirable. Come out into the moonlight. We will
take ten minutes, and then, my dear boy, good-night."

"Good-morning, you mean, mother, and everything
new,—a new life. It has never been as it will be to-morrow.
Have you thought of that?" She gave a sudden pressure
to his arm, and he perceived his folly. "That I should
speak so to you, to whom the greatest change of all has
come!"

"Yes," she said, with a little tremor. "It is to me
that it will make the most difference. And that poor

young creature, so much younger than I, who might be my child!"

"Do you think, when she gets over all this, that it will be much to her? People say——"

"That is a strange question to ask," she said, with agitation,—"a very strange question to ask. When we get over all this,—that is, the shock, and the change, and the awe of the going away,—what will it be then, to all of us? We shall just settle down once more into our ordinary life, as if nothing had happened. That is what will come of it. That is what always comes of it. There is nothing but the common routine, which goes on and on for ever."

She was excited, and shed tears, at which he wondered a little, yet was compassionate of, remembering that she was a woman and worn out. He put his hand upon hers, which lay on his arm. "Poor mother!" he murmured, caressing her hand with his, and feeling all manner of tender cares for her awake in him. Then he added softly, returning in spite of himself to other thoughts, "The force of habit and of the common routine, as you say, cannot be so strong when one is young."

"No," she said; and then, after a pause, "If it is poor Lady Markland you are thinking of, she has her child."

This gave him a certain shock, in the softening of his heart. "The child is the thing I don't like!" he exclaimed, almost sharply. Then he added, "I think the dawn must be near; I feel very chilly. Mother, come in; as you say, it is the best thing not to think, but to go to bed."

CHAPTER VII.

THE morning rose, as they had said to each other, upon a new life.

How strange it is to realise, after the first blow has fallen, that this changed life is still the same! When it brings with it external changes, family convulsions, the alteration of external circumstances, although these secondary things increase the calamity, they give it also a certain natural atmosphere; they are in painful harmony with it. But when the shock, the dreadful business of the moment, is all over, when the funeral has gone away from the doors and the dead has been buried, and everything goes on as before, this commonplace renewal is, perhaps, the most terrible of all to the visionary soul. Minnie and Chatty got out their work,—the coloured work, which they had thought out of place during the first week. They went in the afternoon for a walk, and gathered fresh flowers, as they returned, for the vases in the drawing-room. When evening came they asked Theo if he would not read to them.

It was not a novel they were reading; it was a biography, of a semi-religious character, in which there were a great many edifying letters. They would not, of course, have thought of reading a novel at such a time. Warrender had been wandering about all day, restless, not knowing what to do with himself. He was not given to games of any kind, but he thought to-day that he would have felt something of the sort a relief, though he knew it would have shocked the household. In the afternoon, on a chance suggestion of his mother's, he saw that it was a sort of duty to walk over to Markland and ask how Lady Markland was. Twelve miles—six there and six back again—is a long walk for a student. He sent up his name, and asked whether he could be of any use, but he did not receive encouragement. Lady Markland sent her thanks, and was quite well ("she says," the old butler explained, with a shake of the head, so that no one might believe he agreed in anything so unbecoming). The Honourable John had been telegraphed for, her husband's uncle, and everything was being done; so that there was no need to trouble Mr. Warrender. He went back, scarcely solaced by his walk. He wanted to be doing something. Not Plato; in the circumstances Plato did not answer at all. When he opened his book his thoughts escaped from him, and went off with a bound to matters entirely different. How was it possible that he could give that undivided attention which divine philosophy requires, the day after his father's funeral, the first day of his independent life, the day after——! That extraordinary postscript to the agitations of yesterday told, perhaps, most of all. When the girls asked him to read to them, opening the book at the page where they had left off, and preparing to tell him all that had gone before, so that he might understand the story ("although there is very little story," Minnie said, with satisfaction; "chiefly thoughts upon serious subjects"), he jumped up from his chair in almost fierce rebellion against that sway of the ordinary of which his mother had spoken. "You were right," he said to her; "the common routine is the thing that outlasts everything. I never thought of it before, but it is true."

Mrs. Warrender, though she had herself been quivering with the long-concentrated impatience for which it seemed even now there could be no outlet, was troubled by her son's outburst, and, afraid of what it might come to, felt herself moved to take the other side. "It is very true," she said, faltering a little, "but the common routine is often best for everything, Theo. It is a kind of leading-string, which keeps us going."

The girls looked up at Theo with alarm and wonder, but still they were not shocked at what *he* said. He was a

man; he had come to the Warren from those wild excite-
ments of Oxford life, of which they had heard with awe;
they gazed at him, trying to understand him.

"I have always heard," said Minnie, "that reading
aloud was the most tranquillising thing people could do.
If we had each a book it would be unsociable; but when a
book is read aloud, then we are all thinking about the same
thing, and it draws us together;" which was really the most
sensible judgment that could have been delivered, had the
two fantastic ones been in the mood to understand what
was said.

Chatty did not say anything, but after she had threaded
her needle looked up with great attention to see how the
fate of the evening was to be decided. It was a great
pleasure when some one would read aloud, especially Theo,
who thus became one of them, in a way which was not at
all usual; but perhaps she was less earnest about it this
evening than on ordinary occasions, for the biographical
book was a little dull, and the letters on serious subjects
were dreadfully serious. No doubt, just after papa's death,
this was appropriate; but still it is well known there are
stories which are also serious, and could not do any one
harm, even at the gravest moments.

"There are times when leading-strings are insupport-
able," Theo said; "at any time I don't know that I put

much faith in them. We have much to arrange and settle, mother, if you feel able for it."

"Mamma can't feel able yet," returned Minnie. "Oh, why should we make any change? We are so happy as we are."

"I am quite able," said Mrs. Warrender. She had been schooling herself to the endurance which still seemed to be expected of her, but the moment an outlet seemed possible the light kindled in her eye. "I think with Theo that it is far better to decide whatever has to be done at once." Then she cried out suddenly, carried away by the unexpected unhoped-for opportunity, "O children, we must get away from here! I cannot bear it any longer. As though all our own trouble and sorrow were not enough, this other —this other tragedy!" She put up her hands to her eyes, as though to shut out the sight that pressed upon them. "I cannot get it out of my mind. I suppose my nerves and everything are wrong; all night long it seemed to be before me,—the blood on his forehead, the ghastly white face, the labouring breath. Oh, not like your father, who was good and old and peaceful, who was just taken away gently, led away,—but so young and so unprepared! Oh, so unprepared! What could God do with him, cut off in the midst of——"

Minnie got up hastily, with her smelling-salts, which

always lay on the table. "Go and get her a glass of water,
Theo," she said authoritatively.

Mrs. Warrender laughed. It was a little nervous, but
it was a laugh. It seemed to peal through the house, which
still was a house of mourning, and filled the girls with a
horror beyond words. She put out her hands to put their
ministrations away. "I do not want water," she said, "nor
salts either. I am not going into hysterics. Sit down and
listen to me. I cannot remain here. It is your birthplace,
but not mine. I am dying for fresh air and the sight of the
sun. If you are shocked, I cannot help it. Theo, when you
go back to Oxford I will go to—I don't know where; to
some place where there is more air; but here I cannot
stay."

This statement was as a thunderbolt falling in the midst
of them, and the poor woman perceived this instinctively.
Her son's impatience had been the spark which set the
smouldering fire in her alight, but even he was astounded
by the quick and sudden blaze which lit up the dull wonder
in his sisters' faces. And then he no longer thought of
going to Oxford. He wanted to remain to see if he could
do anything,—perhaps to be of use. A husband's uncle
does not commend himself to one's mind as a very devoted
or useful ministrant, and even he would go away, of course ;
and then a man who was nearer, who was a neighbour, who

had already been so mixed up with the tragedy,—that was what he had been thinking of; not of Oxford, or his work.

" It is not worth while going back to Oxford," he said ; "the term is nearly over. One can read anywhere, at home as well as—I shall not go back at present." He was not accustomed yet to so abrupt a declaration of his sentiments, and for the moment he avoided his mother's eye.

Minnie went back to her seat, and put down the bottle of salts on the table, with an indignant jar. " I am so glad that you feel so, Theo, *too.*"

Mrs. Warrender looked round upon her children with despairing eyes. They were all *his* children,—all Warrenders born ; knowing as little about her and her ways of thinking as if she had been a stranger to them. She was indeed a stranger to them in the intimate sense. The exasperation that had been in her mind for years could be repressed no longer. " If it is so," she said, " I don't wish to interfere with your plans, Theo ; but I will go for—for a little change. I must have it. I am worn out."

" Oh, mamma, you will not surely go by yourself, without us ! How could you get on without us !" cried Chatty. She had perhaps, being the youngest, a faint stir of a feeling in her mind that a little change might be pleasant enough. But she took her mother at her word with this mild protest, which made Mrs. Warrender's impatient cry into a statement of fixed resolution : and the others said nothing. Warrender was silent, because he was absorbed in the new thoughts that filled his mind ; Minnie, because, like Chatty, she felt quite apart from any such extraordinary wishes, having nothing to do with it, and nothing to say.

" It will be very strange, certainly, for me to be alone, —very strange," Mrs. Warrender said, with a quiver in her voice. " It is so long since I have done anything by myself; not since before you were all born. But if it must be," she added, "I must just take courage as well as I can, and—go by myself, as you say."

Once more there was no response. The girls did not know what to say. Duty, they thought, meant staying at home and doing their crewel-work; they were not capable of any other identification of it all at once. It was very strange, but if mamma thought so, what could they do ? She got up with nervous haste, feeling now, since she had once broken bounds, as though the flood of long-restrained feeling was beyond her control altogether. The natural thing would have been to rush upstairs and pack her things, and go off to the railway at once. That, perhaps, might not be practicable ; but neither was it practicable to sit quietly amid the silence and surprise, and see her wild, sudden resolution accepted dully, as if a woman could contemplate such a severance calmly. And yet it was true that she must get fresh air or die. Life so long intolerable could be borne no longer.

"I think in the meantime," she said, with a forced smile, "I shall go upstairs."

"You were up very late last night," returned Theo, though rather by way of giving a sort of sanction to her abrupt withdrawal than for any other reason, as he rose to open the door.

"Yes, it was very late. I think I am out of sorts altogether. And if I am to make my plans without any reference to the rest of the family——"

"Oh, that is absurd," he said. "Of course the girls must go with you, if you are really going. But you must not be in a hurry, mother. There is plenty of time; there is no hurry." He was thinking of the time that must elapse before the doors of Markland would be open even to her who had received Lord Markland into her house. Till then he did not want her to go away. When she had left the room he turned upon his sisters and slew them.

"What do you mean, you two? I wonder if you have got hearts of stone, to hear the poor mother talk of going away for a little change, and to sit there like wooden images, and never open your mouths!"

The girls opened their mouths wide at this unexpected

reproach. "What could we say? Mamma tells us all in a moment she wants to go away from home! We have always been taught that a girl's place is at home."

"What do you call home?" he asked.

It was a brutal speech, he was aware. Brothers and sisters are permitted to be brutal to each other without much harm done. Minnie had begun calmly, with the usual, "Oh, Theo!" before the meaning of the question struck her. She stopped suddenly, looked up at him, with eyes and lips open, with an astonished stare of inquiry. Then, dull though she was, growing red, repeated in a startled, awakened, interrogative tone, "Oh, Theo!" with a little gasp as for breath.

"I don't mean to be disagreeable," he said. "I never should have been, had not you begun. The mother has tried to make you understand half a dozen times, but I suppose you did not want to understand. Don't you know everything is changed since—since I was last at the Warren? Your home is with my mother now, wherever she chooses to settle down."

It must be said for Warrender that he meant no harm whatever by this. He meant, perhaps, to punish them a little for their heartlessness. He meant them to see that their position was changed,—that they were not as of old, in assured possession ; and he reckoned upon that slowness of apprehension which probably would altogether preserve them from any painful consciousness. But it is astonishing how the mind and the senses are quickened when it is ourselves who are in question. Minnie was the leader of the two. She was the first to understand; and then it communicated itself partly by magnetism to Chatty, who woke up much more slowly, having caught as it were only an echo of what her brother said.

"You mean—that this is not our home any more," said Minnie. Her eyes filled with sudden tears, and her face was flushed with the shock. She had seldom looked so well, so thoroughly awakened and mistress of her faculties. When she was roused she had more in her than was apparent on the surface. "I did not think you would be the one to tell us that. Of course we know that it is quite true. Chatty and I are older than you are, but we are only daughters, and you are the boy. You have the power to turn us out,—we all know that."

"Minnie!" cried Chatty, struck with terror, putting out a hand to stop these terrible words,—words such as had never been said in her hearing before.

"But we did not think you would have used it," the elder sister said simply, and then was silent. He expected that she would end the scene by rushing from the room in tears and wrath. But what she did was much more embarrassing. She dried her tears hastily, took up her crewel-work, sat still, and said no more. Chatty threw an indignant but yet at the same time an inquiring glance at him. She had not heard or observed the beginning of the fray, and did not feel quite sure what it was all about.

"I am sure Theo would never do anything that was unkind," she remarked mildly; then after a little pause, "Wouldn't it have been much better to have had the reading? I have noticed that before : when one reads and the others work, there is, as the rector says, a common interest, and we have a nice evening; but when we begin talking instead—well, we think differently, and we disagree, and one says more than one means to say, and then—one is sorry afterwards," Chatty said, after another pause.

On the whole, it was the girls who had the best of it in this encounter. It is impossible to say how much Theo was ashamed of himself when, after Chatty's quite unaccus-tomed address, which surprised herself as much as her brother and sister, and after an hour of silence, broken by an occasional observation, the girls put aside their crewels again, and remarked that it was time to go to bed. A sense of opposition and that pride which prevents a man from being the first to retire from a battle-field, even when the battle is a failure and the main armies have never en-gaged, had kept him there during the evening, in spite of himself. But when they left him master of the ground, there can be no doubt that he felt much more like a defeated than a triumphant general. This first consequence of the new *régime* was not a beautiful or desirable one. There were thus three parties in the house on the evening of the first day of their changed existence : the mother, who was so anxious to leave the scene of her past existence behind her ; the girls, who clung to their home ; the brother, the master, who, half to show that he took his mother's side, half out of instinctive assertion of himself, had let them know roundly that their home was theirs no longer. He was not proud of himself at all as he thought of what he had said ; but yet when he recalled it he was not perhaps so sorry for having said it as he had been the minute after the words left his lips. It was better, possibly, as the lawyer, as the mother, as everybody, had said, that the true state of affairs should be fully understood from the first. The house was theirs no longer. The old reign and all its traditions had passed away ; a new reign had begun. What that new reign might turn to, who might share it, what wonderful developments it might take, who could tell ?

His imagination here went away with a leap into realms of sheer romance. He seemed to see the old house trans- formed, the free air, the sweet sunshine pouring in, the homely rooms made beautiful, the inhabitants—— What was he thinking of? Did ever imagination go so fast or so far? He stopped himself, with vague smiles stealing to his lips. All that enchanted ground was so new to him that he had no control over his fancy, but went to the utmost length with a leap of bewildering pleasure and daring almost like a child. Yet mingled with this were various elements which were not lovely. He was not, so far as had been previously apparent, selfish beyond the natural liking for his own comfort and his own way, which is almost universal. He had never wished to cut himself off from his family, or to please himself at their expense. But something had come into his mind which is nearer than the nearest,—something which, with a new and un-comprehended fire, hardens the heart on one side while melting it on the other, and brings tenderness undreamed of and cruelty impossible to be believed, from the same source. He felt the conflict of these powers within him when he was left alone in the badly furnished, badly lighted drawing-room, which seemed to reproach him for the retire-ment of those well-known figures which had filled it with tranquil dulness for so many years, and never wished it different. With something of the same feeling towards the inanimate things about him which he had expressed to his sisters, he walked up and down the room. It too would have to change, like them, to acknowledge that he was

master, to be moulded to new requirements. He felt as
if the poor old ugly furniture, the hard curtains that hung
like pieces of painted wood, the dingy pictures on the
walls, contemplated him with pain and disapproval. They
were easier to deal with than the human furniture; but he
had been accustomed to them all his life, and it was not
without a sense of impiety that the young iconoclast contemplated these grim household gods, harmless victims of
that future which as yet was but an audacious dream. He
was standing in front of the great chiffonnier, with its marble
top and plate-glass back, looking with daring derision at its
ugliness, when old Joseph came in at his usual hour—the
hour at which he had fulfilled the same duty for the last
twenty years—to put out the lamps. Warrender could
horrify the girls and insult the poor old familiar furniture,
but he was not yet sufficiently advanced to defy Joseph. He
turned round, with a blush and quick movement of shame,
as if he had been found out, at the appearance of the old
man with his candle in his hand, and murmuring something
about work, hurried off to the library, with a fear that even
that refuge might perhaps be closed upon him. Joseph
remained master of the situation. He followed Warrender
to the door with his eyes, with a slight contemptuous shrug
of his shoulders, as at an unaccountable being whose
" ways " were scarcely important enough to be taken into

account, and trotted about, putting out one lamp after
another, and the twinkling candles on the mantelpiece, and
the little lights in the hall and corridor. It was an office
Joseph liked. He stood for a moment at the foot of the
back stairs looking with complacency upon the darkness,
his candle lighting up his little old wry face. But when
his eye caught the line of light under the library door,
Joseph shook his head. He had put the house to bed
without disturbance for so long: he could not abide, he
said to himself, this introduction of new ways.

CHAPTER VIII

It was a violent beginning ; but perhaps it was as well, on the whole, that the idea of Theo's future supremacy should have been got into the heads of the duller portion of the family. Warrender was so anxious that there should be no unnecessary haste in his mother's departure, and so ready to find out a pleasant place where they could all go, that everything that had been harsh was forgotten. Indeed, it is very possible in a family that a great many harsh things may be said and forgotten, with little harm done—boys and girls who have been brought up in the same nursery having generally insulted as well as caressed each other with impunity from their earliest years. This happy effect of the bonds of nature was no doubt made easier by the placid characters of the girls, who had no inclination to brood over an unkindness, nor any habit of thinking what was meant by a hasty word. On the contrary, when they remembered it in the morning, after their sound night's sleep, they said to each other that Theo could not possibly have meant it; that he must have been out of temper, poor fellow. They even consented to listen and to look when, with unusual amiability, he called them out to see what trees he intended to cut down, and what he meant to do. Minnie and Chatty indeed bewailed every individual tree, and kissed the big, tottering old elm, which had menaced the nursery window since ever they could remember, and shut out the light. "Dear old thing!" they said, shedding a tear or two upon its rough bark. "It would be dear indeed if it brought down the wall and smashed the old play-room," their brother said,—an argument which even to these natural conservatives bore, now that the first step had been taken, a certain value. Sometimes it is not amiss to go too far when the persons you mean to convince are a little obtuse. They entered into the question almost with warmth at last. The flower garden would be so much improved, for one thing; there never had been sun enough for the flowers, and the big trees had taken, the gardener said, all the goodness out of the soil. Perhaps after all Theo might be right. Of course he knew so much more of the world!

"And, mother, before you go, you should see—Lady Markland," Theo said.

There was a little hesitation in his voice before he pronounced the name, but of this no one took any notice, at the time.

"I have been wondering what I should do. There has been no intimacy, not more than acquaintanceship."

"After what has happened you surely cannot call yourselves mere acquaintances, you and she."

"Perhaps not that : but it is not as if she had thrown herself upon my sympathy, Theo. She was very self-contained. Nobody could doubt that she felt it dreadfully ; but she did not fling herself upon me, as many other women would have done."

"I should not think that was at all her character," said Warrender.

"No, I don't suppose it is her character ; and then there were already two of her, so to speak,—that child——"

"The only thing I dislike in her," he said hastily, "is that child. What good can a creature of that age do her? And it must be so bad for the boy."

"I don't know about the good it can do her. You don't any of you understand," Mrs. Warrender said, with a moistening of her eyes, "the good there is in a child. As young people grow up they become more important, no doubt,—oh yes, far more important,—and take their own place. But a little thing that belongs to you, that has no thoughts but what are your thoughts, that never wants to be away from you——"

"Very unnatural," said the young man severely, "or

else fictitious. The little thing, you may be sure, would much rather be playing with its own companions; or else it must be an unhealthy little sentimental——"

Mrs. Warrender shook her head, but said no more. She gave him a look half remonstrating, half smiling. I had a little boy once, it was on her lips to say: but she forbore. How was the young man, beginning his own individual career, thinking of everything in the world rather than of such innocent consolation as can be given to a woman by a child, to understand that mystery? She whose daughters, everybody said, must be "such companions," and her son "such a support," looked back wistfully upon the days when they were little children; but then she was an unreasonable woman. She was roused from a little visionary journey back into her own experiences by the sound of Theo's voice going on :—

"——should call and ask," he was saying. "She might want you. She must want some one, and they say she has no relations. I think certainly you should call and ask. Shall I order the brougham for you this afternoon? I would drive you over myself, but perhaps, in the circumstances, it would be more decorous——"

"It must be the brougham; if you think I ought to go so soon——"

"Well, mother, you are the best judge; but I suppose

that if women can be of any use to each other it must be at such a—at a time when other people are shut out."

Mrs. Warrender was much surprised by his fervour : but she remembered that her husband had been very punctilious about visiting, as men in the country often are, the duty of keeping up all social connections falling upon their wives, and not on themselves. The brougham was ordered, accordingly, and she set out alone, though Minnie would willingly have strained a point to accompany her. "Don't you think, mamma, that as I am much nearer her own age she might like me to go?'' that young lady said. But here Theo came in again with his newly acquired authority. "Mother is the right person," he said.

She did not feel much like the right person as she drove along. Lady Markland had not wanted consolation ; the shock had turned her to stone. And then she had her child, and seemed to need no other minister. But if it pleased Theo, that was motive enough. Mrs. Warrender reflected, as she pursued her way, upon the kind of squire he would make, different from his father,—oh, very different ; not the ordinary type of the English country gentleman. He would not hunt, he would shoot very little ; but her husband had not been enthusiastic in either of these pursuits. He would not care, perhaps, for county business or for the

quarter sessions ; he would have too much contempt for the
country bumpkins to be popular with the farmers or wield
political influence. Very likely (she thought), he would
not live much at the Warren, but keep rooms at Oxford, or
perhaps go to London. She had no fear that he would ever
"go wrong."   That was as great an impossibility as that
he should be prime minister or Archbishop of Canterbury.
But yet it was a little odd that he should be so particular
about keeping up the accidental connection with Lady
Markland.   This showed that he was not so indifferent to
retaining his place in the county and keeping up all local
ties as she thought.   As for any other ideas that Theo
might associate with the young widow,—the widow whose
husband lay still unburied,—nothing of the kind entered
Mrs. Warrender's head.

The nakedness of the house seemed to be made more
conspicuous by the blank of all the closed windows, the
white blinds down, the white walls shining like a sort of
colourless monument in the blaze of the westering sun.
The sound of the wheels going up the open road which was
called an avenue seemed a kind of insult to the stillness
which brooded over the house of death.   When the old
butler came solemnly down the great steps, the small country
lady, who was not on Lady Markland's level, felt her little
pretence at intimacy quite unjustifiable.   The butler came

down the steps with a solemn air to receive a card and
inquiries, and to give the stereotyped reply that her lady-
ship was as well as could be looked for : but lifted astonished
eyes, not without a gleam of insolence in them, when Mrs.
Warrender made the unexpected demand if Lady Markland
would see her.   See *you !*   If it had been the duchess,
perhaps ! was the commentary legible in his face.   He
went in, however, with the card in his hand, while she
waited, half indignant, half amused, with little doubt what
the reply would be.   But the reply was not at all what she
expected.   After a minute or two of delay, another figure,
quite different from that of the butler, appeared on the steps :
a tall man, with very thin, unsteady legs, a face on which
the ravages of age were visibly repaired by many devices
unknown to its simpler victims, with an eye-glass in his eye
and a hesitation in his speech.   He was not unknown to
the society about, though he showed himself but rarely in
it, and was not beloved when he appeared.   He was Lord
Markland's uncle, the late lord's only brother,—he who was
supposed to have led the foolish young man astray.   Mrs.
Warrender looked at him with a certain horror, as he came
walking gingerly down the steps.   He made a very elaborate
bow at the carriage door,—if he were really Satan in person,
as many people thought, he was a weak-kneed Satan,—and
gulped and stammered a good deal (in which imperfections

we need not follow him) as he made his compliments.   His
niece, he said, had charged him with the kindest messages,
but she was ill and lying down.   Would Mrs. Warrender
excuse her for to-day?

"She is most grateful for so much kindness; and there
is a favour—ah, a favour which I have to ask.   It is, if you
would add to your many kind services———"

"I have rendered no kind services, Mr. Markland.
The accident happened at our doors."

"Ah, no less kind for that.   My niece is very grateful,
and I—and I, too,—that goes without saying.   If we
might ask you to come to-morrow, to remain with her
while the last rites———"

"To remain with her!   Are you sure that is Lady
Markland's wish?"

"My dear lady, it is mine, and hers,—hers, too; again,
that goes without saying.   She has no relations.   She wants
countenance,—countenance and support; and who could
give them so fitly as yourself?   In the same circumstances :
accept my sincerest regrets.   Mr. Warrender was, I have
alway heard, an excellent person, and must be a great loss.
But you have a son, I think."

"Yes, I have a son."

"Who has been here twice to inquire?   Most friendly,
most friendly, I am sure.   I see, therefore, that you take

an interest—Then may we calculate upon you, Wednesday, as early as will suit you?"

"I will come," said Mrs. Warrender, still hesitating, "if you are quite sure it is Lady Markland's wish."

While he repeated his assurances, another member of the family appeared at the door, little Geoff, in a little black dress, which showed his paleness, his meagre, small person, insignificance, and sickliness more than ever. He had been there, it would seem, looking on while his uncle spoke. At this moment he came down deliberately, one step at a time, till his head was on a level with the carriage window. "It is quite true," he said. "Mother's in her own room. She's tired, but she wants you, if you'll come; anyhow, *I* want you, please, if you'll come. They say I'm to go, but not mamma : and you know she couldn't be left by herself; uncle thinks so, and so do I."

The little thing stood shuffling from one foot to another, his hands in his pockets, his little gray eyes looking everywhere but at the compassionate face turned to him from the carriage window. There was a curious ridiculous repetition in the child's attitude of Theo's assertion of his rights. But Mrs. Warrender's heart was soft to the child. "I don't think she wants me," she said. "I will do anything at such a time, but——"

"I want you," said Geoff. He gave her a momentary

glance, and she could see that the little colourless eyes had
tears in them. " I shall have to go and leave her, and
who will take care of her ? She is to have a thing like
yours upon her head." He was ready to sob, but kept
himself in with a great effort, swallowing the little convulsion of nature. His mother's widow's cap was more to
Geoff than his father's death ; at least it was a visible sign
of something tremendous which had happened, more telling
than the mere absence of one who had been so often absent.
" Come, Mrs. Warrender," he said, with a hoarseness of
passion in his little voice. " I can leave her if you are
there."

" I will come for your sake, Geoff," she said, holding out
her hand, and with tears in her eyes. He was not big
enough to reach it from where he stood, and the tears in her
voice affected the little hero. He dug his own hands deeper
into his pockets, and shuffled off without any reply. It
was the uncle, whose touch she instinctively shrank from,
who took and bowed over Mrs. Warrender's hand. The
Honourable John bowed over it as if he were about to kiss
it, and might have actually touched the black glove with
his carmine lips (would they have left a mark ?) had not she
drawn it away.

What a curious office to be thus imposed upon her !
To give countenance and support, or to take care of, as

little Geoff said, this young woman whom she scarcely knew, who had not in the depth of trouble made any claim upon her sympathy. Mrs. Warrender looked forward with anything but satisfaction to the task. But when she told her tale it was received with a sort of enthusiasm. "Oh, how nice of her!" cried Minnie and Chatty; and their mother saw, with half amusement, that they thought all the more of her because her companionship had been sought for by Lady Markland. And in Warrender's eyes a fire lighted up. He turned away his head, and after a moment said, "You will be very tender to her, mother." Mrs. Warrender was too much confused and bewildered to make any reply.

When the next day came she went, with reluctance and a sense of self-abnegation, which was not gratifying, but painful, to fulfil this office. "She does not want me, I know," Mrs. Warrender said to her son, who accompanied her, to form part of the cortége, in the little brougham which had been to Markland but once or twice in so many years, and this last week had traversed the road from one house to another almost every day. "I think you are mistaken, mother; but even so, if you can do her any good," said Theo, with unusual enthusiasm. His mother thought it strange that he should show so much feeling on the subject; and she went through the great hall and up

the stairs, through the depths of the vast silent house, to
Lady Markland's room, with anticipations as little agreeable
as any with which woman ever went to an office of kindness.   Lady Markland's room was on the other side of the
house, looking upon a landscape totally different from that
through which her visitor had come.   The window was
open, the light unshaded, and Lady Markland sat at a
writing-table covered with papers, as little like a broken-
hearted widow as could be supposed.   She was dressed,
indeed, in the official dress of heavy crape, and wore (for
once) the cap which to Geoff had been so overpowering a
symbol of sorrow ; but, save for these signs, and perhaps a
little additional paleness in her never high complexion, was
precisely as Mrs. Warrender had seen her since she had
risen from her girlish bloom into the self-possession of a
wife, matured and stilled by premature experience.   She
came forward, holding out her hand, when her visitor, with
a reluctance and diffidence quite unsuitable to her superior
age, slowly advanced.

"Thank you," she said at once, "for coming.   I know
without a word how disagreeable it is to you, how little
you wished it.   You have come against your will, and you
think against my will, Mrs. Warrender ; but indeed it is not
so.   It is a comfort and help to me to have you."

"If that is so, Lady Markland——"

"That is why you have come," she said. "It is so. I know you have come unwillingly. You heard—they have taken the boy from me."

"But only for this day."

"Only for the hour, I hope. It is supposed to be too much for me to go." Here she smiled, with a nervous movement of her face. "Nothing is too much for me. You know a little about it, but not all. Do you remember him when we were married, Mrs. Warrender? I recollect you were one of the first people I saw."

This sudden plunge into the subject for which she was least prepared—for all her ideas of condolence had been driven out of her mind by the young woman's demeanour, the open window, the cheerful and common-place air of the room—confused Mrs. Warrender greatly. "I remember Lord Markland almost all his life," she said.

"Here is the miniature of him that was done for me before we were married," said Lady Markland, rising hurriedly, and bringing it from the table. "Look at it; did you ever see a more hopeful face? He was so fresh; he was so full of spirits. Who could have thought there was any canker in that face?"

"There was not then," said the elder woman, looking through a mist of natural tears—the tears of that profound regret for a life lost which are more bitter, almost, than

personal sorrow—at the miniature. She remembered him
so well, and how everybody thought all would come right
with the poor young fellow when he was so happily married
and had a home.

"Ah, but there was!—nobody told me; though if all
the world had told me it would not have made any difference. Mrs. Warrender, he is like that now. Everything
else is gone. He looks as he did at twenty, as good and
as pure. What do you think it means? Does it mean
anything? Or is there only some physical interpretation
of it, as these horrible men say?"

"My dear," said Mrs. Warrender, quite subdued, "they
say it means that all is pardoned, and that they have
entered into peace."

"Peace," she said. "I was afraid you were going to
say rest; and he who had never laboured wanted no rest.
Peace,—where the wicked cease from troubling, is that
what you mean? He had no time to repent."

"My dear—oh, I am not clear, I can't tell you; but
who can tell what was in his mind between the time he
saw his danger and the blow that stunned him? If my
boy had done everything against me, and all in a moment
turned and called to me, would I refuse him? And is not
God," cried one mother to the other, taking her hands,
"better than we?"

It was she who had come to be the comforter who wept, tears streaming down her cheeks. The other held her hands, and looked in her face with dry feverish eyes. " Your boy," she said slowly, " he is good and kind,—he is good and kind. Will my boy be like him? Or do you think there is an inheritance in that as in other things?"

CHAPTER IX.

THE post town for the Warren was Highcombe, which was
about four miles off. To drive there had always been
considered a dissipation, not to say a temptation, for the
Warrenders ; at least for the feminine portion of the family.
There were at Highcombe what the ladies called "quite
good shops,"—shops where you could get everything, really
as good as town, and if not cheaper, yet still quite as cheap,
if you added on the railway fare and all the necessary
expenses you were inevitably put to, if you went to town on
purpose to shop. Accordingly, it was considered prudent
to go to Highcombe as seldom as possible ; only when there
was actually something wanted, or important letters to post,
or such a necessity as balanced the probable inducement
to buy things that were not needed, or spend money that
might have been spared. The natural consequence of this
prudential regulation was that the little shop in the village
which lay close to their gates had been encouraged to keep
sundry kinds of goods not usually found in a little village

shop, and that Minnie and Chatty very often passed that
way in their daily walks. Old Mrs. Bagley had a good
selection of shaded Berlin wools and a few silks, and even,
when the fashion came in for that, crewels. She had a few
Berlin patterns, and pieces of muslin stamped for that
other curious kind of ornamentation which consisted in
cutting holes and sewing them round. And she had beads
of different sizes and colours, and in short quite a little
case of things intended for the occupation of that super-
abundant leisure which ladies often have in the country.
In the days with which we are concerned there were not
so many activities possible as now. The village and parish
were not so well looked after. There was no hospital
nearer than the county hospital at Highcombe, and the
" Union " was in the parish of Standingby, six miles off, too
far to be visited ; neither had it become the fashion then
to visit hospitals and workhouses. The poor of the village
were poor neighbours. The sick were nursed, with more
or less advantage, at home. Beef-tea and chicken broth
flowed from the Warren, whenever it was necessary, into
whatsoever cottage stood in need, and very good, wholesome calf's-foot jelly, though perhaps not quite so clear as
that which came from the Highcombe confectioners. Everything was done in a neighbourly way, without organisation.
Perhaps it was better, perhaps worse. In human affairs it

is always so difficult to make certain. But at all events
the young ladies had not so much to do. And lawn tennis
had not been yet invented, croquet even was but in the
mild fervour of its first existence. Schools of cookery and
ambulances were unknown. And needle-work, bead-work,
muslin-work, flourished. Crochet, even, was still pursued
as a fine-art occupation. That period is as far back as the
Crusades to the sympathetic reader, but to the Miss Warrenders it was the natural state of affairs. They went to
Mrs. Bagley's very often, in the dulness of the afternoon,
to turn over the Berlin wools and the crochet cottons, to
match a shade, or to find a size they wanted. The expen-
diture was not great, and it gave an object to their walk.
" I must go out," they would say to each other, " for there
is that pink to match ;" or " I shall be at a stand-still with
my antimacassar ; my cotton is almost done." It was not
the fault of Minnie and Chatty that they had nothing better
to do.

Mrs. Bagley was old, but very lively, and capable, even
while selling soap, or sugar, or a piece of bacon, or a tin
tea-kettle, of seeing through her old spectacles whether the
tint selected was one that matched. She was a woman
who had "come through" much in her life. Her children
were all grown up, and most of them dead. Those who
remained were married, with children of their own, making

a great struggle to bring them up, as she herself had done in her day. She had two daughters, widows,—one in the village, one at some distance off; and living with herself, dependent on her, yet not dependent altogether, was all that remained of another daughter, the one supposed to have been her favourite. It seemed to the others rather hard that granny should lavish all her benefits upon Eliza, while their own families got only little presents and helps now and then. But Lizzie was always the one with mother, they said, though goodness knows she had cost enough in her lifetime without leaving such a charge on granny's hands. Lizzie Bagley, who in her day had been the prettiest of the daughters, had married out of her own sphere, though it could not be said to be a very grand marriage. She had married a clerk, a sort of gentleman,— not like the ploughman and country tradesman who had fallen to the lot of her sisters. But he had never done well, had lost one situation after another, and had gone out finally to Canada, where he died,—he and his wife both; leaving their girl with foreign ways and a will of her own, such as the aunts thought (or at least said) does not develop on the home soil. As poor little Lizzie, however, had been but two years away, perhaps the blame did not entirely lie with Canada. Her mother's beauty and her father's gentility had given to Lizzie many advantages over her cousins.

She was prettier and far more "like a lady" than the best of them ; she had a slim, straight little person, without the big joints and muscles of the race, and with blue eyes which were really blue, and not whitey-gray. And instead of going out to service, as would have been natural, she had learned dressmaking, which was a fine-lady sort of a trade, and put nonsense into her head, and led her into vanity. To see her in the sitting-room behind the shop, with her hair so smooth and her waist so small and collars and cuffs as nice as any young lady's, was as gall and wormwood to the mothers of girls quite as good (they said) as Lizzie, and just as near to granny, but never cosseted and petted in that way. And what did granny expect was to become of her at the end ? So long as she was sure of her 'ome, and so long as the young ladies at the Warren gave her a bit of work now and again, and Mrs. Wilberforce at the Rectory had her in to make the children's things, all might be well enough. But the young ladies would marry, and the little Wilberforces would grow up, and granny—well, granny could not expect to live for ever. And what would Miss Lizzie do then ? This was what the aunts would say, shaking their heads. Mrs. Bagley, when she said any-thing at all in her own defence, declared that poor little Lizzie had no one to look to her, neither father nor mother, and that if her own granny didn't take her up and do for her, who should? And that, besides, she did very well with her dressmaking. But nevertheless, by time, Mrs. Bagley had her own apprehensions too.

Minnie and Chatty were fond of making expeditions into the shop, as has been said. They liked to have a talk with Lizzie, and to turn over her fashion-books, old and new, and perhaps to plan, next time they had new frocks, how the sleeves should be made. It was a pleasant "object" for their walk, a break in the monotony, and gave them something to talk about. They went in one afternoon, shortly after the events which have been described. Chatty had occasion for a strip of muslin stamped for working, to complete some of her new underclothing which she had been making. The shop had one large square window, in which a great many different kinds of wares were exhibited, from bottles full of barley sugar and acid drops to bales of striped stuff for petticoats. Bunches of candles dangled from the roof, and nets of onions, and the old lady herself was weighing an ounce of tea for one of her poor customers when the young ladies came in. " Is Lizzie at home, Mrs. Bagley?" said Minnie. " Don't mind us,—we can look for what we want; and you mustn't let your other customers wait."

" You're always that good, miss," said the old woman. Her dialect could only be expressed by much multiplication of vowels, and would not be a satisfactory representation even then, so that it is not necessary to trouble the eye of the reader with its peculiarities. A certain amount of this pronunciation may be taken for granted. "If all the quality would be as considerate, it would be a fine thing for poor folks."

"Oh, but people with any sense would always be considerate! How is your mother, Sally? Is it for her you are buying the tea? Cocoa is very nourishing; it is an excellent thing for her."

"If you please, miss," said Sally, who was the purchaser, "mother do dearly love a cup of tea."

"You ought to tell her that the cocoa is far more nourishing," said Minnie. "It would do her a great deal more good."

"Ah, miss, but there isn't the heart in it that there is in a cup o' tea," said Mrs. Bagley. "It do set a body up when so be as you're low. Coffee and cocoa and that's fine and warming of a morning; but when the afternoon do come, and you feels low———"

"Why should you feel low more in the afternoon than in the morning, Mrs. Bagley? There's no reason in that."

"Ain't there, miss? There's a deal of 'uman nature, though. Not young ladies like you, that have everything as you want; but even my Lizzie, I find as she wants her tea badly afternoons."

"And so do we," said Chatty, "especially when we don't go out. Look here, this is just the same as the last we had. Mrs. Wilberforce had such a pretty pattern yesterday,—a pattern that made a great deal of appearance, and yet went so quick in working. She had done a quarter of a yard in a day."

"You'll find it there, miss," said the old woman. "Mrs. Wilberforce don't get her patterns nowhere but from me. Lizzie chose it herself, last time she went to High-combe. And they all do say as the child has real good taste, better nor many a lady. Lizzie! Why, here's the young ladies, and you never showing. Lizzie, child! She's terribly taken up with a—with a—no, I can't call it a job,—with an offer she's had."

"An offer! Do you mean a real *offer?*" cried the girls together, with excitement, both in a breath.

"Oh, not a hoffer of marriage, miss, if that's what you're thinking of, though she's had them too. This is just as hard to make up her mind about. Not to me," said the old woman. "But perhaps I've give her too much of her own way, and now when I says, Don't, she up and says, Why, granny? It ain't always so easy to say why; but when your judgment's agin it, without no reason,

I'm always for following the judgment. Lizzie! Perhaps, miss, you'd give her your advice."

Lizzie came out, as this was said, through the little glass door, with a little muslin curtain veiling the lower panes, which opened into the room beyond. She made a curtsey, as in duty bound, to the young ladies, but she said with some petulance, "I ain't deaf, granny," as she did so.

"She has always got her little word to say for herself," the old woman replied, with a smile. She had opened the glass case which held the muslin patterns, and was turning them over with the tips of her fingers,—those fingers which had so many different kinds of goods to touch, and were not, perhaps, adapted for white muslin. "Look at this one, miss; it's bluebells that is, just for all the world like the bluebells in the woods in the month o' May."

"I've got the new Moniture, Miss Warrender, and there are some sweet things in it,—some sweetly pretty things," said Lizzie, holding up her paper. Minnie and Chatty, though they were such steady girls, were not above being fluttered by the Moniteur de la Mode. They both abandoned the muslin-work, and passed through the little door of the counter which Mrs. Bagley held open for them. The room behind, though perhaps not free from a little perfume of the cheese and bacon which occupied the back part of the shop, was pleasant enough; it had a broad lattice win-

dow, looking over the pleasant fields, under which stood
Lizzie's work-table, a large white wooden one, very clean
and old, with signs of long scrubbing and the progress of
time, scattered over with the little litter of dressmaking.
The floor was white deal, very clean also, with a bit of
bright-coloured carpet under Lizzie's chair.   As it was
the sitting-room and kitchen and all, there was a little fire
in the grate.

"Now," said Mrs. Bagley, coming in after them and
shutting the door, for there was no very lively traffic in the
shop, "the young ladies is young like yourself, not to take
too great a liberty, and you think as I'm old and old-
fashioned.   Just you tell the young ladies straight off, and
see what they'll say."

"It ain't of such dreadful consequence, granny.   A
person would think my life depended on it to hear you
speak.   Sleeves are quite small this summer, as I said
they would be; and if you'll look at this trimming, Miss
Chatty, it is just the right thing for crape."

"People don't wear crape, Miss Muffler tells us, nearly
so much as they used to do," said Miss Warrender, "or at
least not nearly so long as they used to do.   Six months,
she says, for a parent."

"Your common dresses will be worn out by then, miss,"
said Lizzie.   "I wouldn't put any on your winter frocks,

if I was you, for black materials are always heavy, and crape don't show on those thick stuffs. I'd just have a piping for the best, and——"

"What's that," said Chatty, who was the most curious, "that has such a strong scent—and gilt-edged paper? You must have got some very grand correspondent, Lizzie."

Lizzie made a hasty movement to secure a letter which lay on the table, and looked as if about to thrust it into her pocket. She changed her mind, however, with a slight scowl on her innocent-seeming countenance, and, reluctantly unfolding it, showed the date in large gilt letters: "The Elms, Underwood, Highcombe." Underwood was the name of the village. Minnie and Chatty repeated it aloud; and one recoiled a few steps, while the other turned upon Lizzie with wide-open, horrified eyes. "The Elms! Lizzie, you are not going there!"

"That's what I say, miss," cried Mrs. Bagley with delight; "that's what I tells her. Out o' respect to her other customers she couldn't go there!"

"To the Elms!" repeated Minnie. She became pale with the horror of the idea. "I can only say, Lizzie, in that case, that mamma would certainly never employ you again. Charlotte and I might be sorry as having known you all our lives, but we could do nothing against mamma. And Mrs. Wilberforce too," she added. "You may be

sure she would do the same. The Elms—why, no respectable person—I should think not even the Vidlers and the
Drivers——"

"That is what I tells her, miss,—that's exactly what
I tells her—nobody—much less madam at the Warren, or
the young ladies as you're so fond of : that's what I tells her
every day."

Lizzie, whose forehead had been puckered up all this
time into a frown, which entirely changed the character of
her soft face, here declared with some vehemence that she
had never said she was going to the Elms,—never! Though
when folks asked her civilly, and keeping a lady's-maid and
all, and dressing beautiful, and nothing proved against them,
who was she that she should say she wouldn't go? "And
I thought it might be such a good thing for granny, who is
always complaining of bad times, if she could get their
custom. It's a house where nothing isn't spared," said
Lizzie ; "even in the servants' hall the best tea and everything." She was fond of the young ladies, but at such an
opportunity not to give them a gentle blow in passing was
beyond the power of woman ; for not even in the drawing-
room did the gentlefolks at the Warren drink the best tea.

"I wouldn't have their custom, not if it was offered to
me," said Mrs. Bagley with vehemence. "And everybody
knows as every single thing they have comes from High-

combe, if not London. I hope as they mayn't find an empty nest some fine morning, and all the birds away. It would serve that nasty Molasis right, as is always taking the bread out of country folk's mouth."

" That's just what I was thinking, granny," said the girl. " If I'd gone it would have been chiefly for your sake. But since the young ladies and you are both so set against it, I can't, and there's an end."

" I am sure she never meant it," said the younger sister. " She was only just flattered for a moment, weren't you, Lizzie? and pleased to think of some one new."

" That's about the fact, that is," said the old woman. " Something new; them lasses would just give their souls for something new."

" But Lizzie must know," said Miss Warrender, " that her old customers would never stand it. I was going to talk about some work, and of coming up two days next week to the Warren. But if there is any idea of the—other place——"

" For goodness' sake speak up and say, No, miss, there ain't no thought of it, Lizzie!"

" Now I know you're so strong against it, of course I can't, and there's an end," said Lizzie; but she looked more angry than convinced.

CHAPTER X.

THE girls went round by the rectory on their way home. It was a large red brick house, taller almost than the church, which was a very old church, credibly dating from the thirteenth century, with a Norman arch to the chancel, which tourists came to see. The rectory was of the days of Anne, three stories high, with many twinkling windows in framework of white, and a great deal of ivy and some livelier climbing plants covering the walls, with the old mellow red bricks looking through the interstices of all this greenery. The two Miss Warrenders did not stop to knock or ring, but opened the door from the outside, and went straight through the house, across the hall and a passage at the other end, to the garden beyond, where Mrs. Wilberforce sat under some great limes, with her little tea-table beside her. She was alone; that is, as near alone as she ever was, with only two of the little ones playing at her feet, and the little Skye comfortably disposed on the cushions of a low wicker-work chair. The two sisters

kissed her, and disturbed the children's game to kiss them,
and displaced the little Skye, who did not like it at all.
Mrs. Wilberforce was a little roundabout woman, with fair
hair and a permanent pucker in her forehead. She was
very well off,—she and all her belongings; the living was
good, the parish small, the work not overpowering: but
she never was able to shake off a visionary anxiety, the
burden of some ancestral trouble, or the premonition of
something to come. She was always afraid that something
was going to happen : her husband to break down from
overwork (which for clergymen, as for most other people
in this generation, is the fashionable complaint), the parish
to be invaded with dissent and socialism, the country to go
to destruction. This latter, as being the greatest, and at
the same time the most distant, a thing even which might
happen without disturbing one's individual comfort, was
most certain ; and she waited till it should happen, with
always an anxious outlook for the first symptoms. She
received Minnie and Chatty, who were her nearest neighbours, and whom she saw almost daily, with a tone of
interest and attachment beyond the ordinary, as she had
done ever since their father's death. Indeed, they had
found this everywhere, a sort of natural compensation for
their "great loss." They were surrounded by the respect
and reawakened interest of all the people who were so

familiar with them. A bereaved family have always this little advantage after a death.

"How are you, dears," Mrs. Wilberforce said, "and how is your dear mother?" Ordinarily Mrs. Warrender was spoken of as their mother, *tout court*, without any endearing adjective.

"Mamma is quite wonderful," said Minnie. "She thinks of everything and looks after everything almost as if—nothing had ever happened."

"She keeps up on our account," said Chatty, "and for Theo's sake. It is so important, you know, to keep home a little bright—oh, I mean as little miserable as possible for him."

"Bright, poor child!" said Mrs. Wilberforce pathetically. "You have not realised as yet what it is. When the excitement is all over, and you have settled down in your mourning, then is the time when you will feel it. I always tell people the first six weeks is nothing; you are so supported by the excitement. But afterwards, when everything falls into the old routine. I suppose, however, you are going away."

"Mamma said something about it : but we all preferred, you know——"

"You had much better go away. I told you so the moment I heard it. And as Theo has all the summer to himself before he requires to go back to Oxford, what is there to stop you?"   Mrs. Wilberforce took great pleasure in settling other people's plans for them, and deciding what they were to do.

" That wasn't what we came to talk about," said the elder Miss Warrender, who was quite able to hold her own. " Mrs. Wilberforce, we have just come from old Mrs. Bagley's at the shop, and there we made quite a painful discovery.   We said what we could, but perhaps it would be well if you would interfere.   I think, indeed, you ought to interfere with authority, or even, perhaps, the rector."

" What is it?   I always thought that old body had a turn for Dissent.   She will have got one of those people from Highcombe to come out and hold a meeting : that is how they always begin."

" Oh no,—a great deal worse than that."

" Minnie means worse in our way of thinking," the younger sister explained.

" I don't know anything worse," said the clergyman's wife, " than the bringing in of Dissent to a united parish such as ours has been.   But I know it will come.   I am always expecting to hear of it every day ; things go so fast nowadays.   What with radicalism, and the poor people all having votes, and what you call progress, one never knows what to expect, except the worst.   I always

look for the worst.   Well, what is it then, if it isn't
Dissent ?"

Then Miss Warrender gave an account of the real state
of affairs.   "The letter was there on the table, dated the
Elms, Underwood, Highcombe, as if—as if it was a county
family ; just as we put it ourselves on our paper."

" But far finer than ours,—gilt, and paper so polished
and shining, and a quarter of an inch thick.   Oh, much
finer than ours !"

"Ours, of course, will be black-edged for a long, long
time to come; there could not be any comparison," said
Minnie, with a sigh.   " But think of the assurance of such
people !   I am so glad to have found you alone, for we
couldn't have talked about it before the rector.   And I
believe if we hadn't gone there just at the right moment
she would have accepted.   I told her mamma would never
employ her again."

" I never had very much opinion of that little thing,"
said Mrs. Wilberforce.   " She is a great deal too fine.   If
her grandmother was a sensible person, she would have
put a stop to all those feathers and flowers and things."

" Still," said Minnie, with some severity, " a young woman
who is a dressmaker and gets the fashion-books, and is perhaps in the way of temptation, may wear a feather in her
hat ; but that is not to say that she should encourage im-

morality, and make for anybody who asks her: especially
considering the way we have all taken her up."

" Who is it that encourages immorality?" said a different
voice, over Mrs. Wilberforce's head,—quite a different voice;
a man's voice, for one thing, which always changes the
atmosphere a little.   It was the rector himself, who came
across the lawn in the ease of a shooting-coat, with his
hands in his pockets.   He wore a long coat when he went
out in the parish, but at home there can be no doubt that
he liked to be at his ease.   He was a man who was too
easy in general, and might, perhaps, if his wife had not
scented harm from the beginning, have compromised himself by calling at the Elms.

"Oh, please!" cried Minnie, with a blush.   "Mrs.
Wilberforce will tell you.   We really have not time to stay
any longer.   Not any tea, thank you.   We must be running away."

" There is nothing to be so sensitive about," said the
clergyman's wife.   " Of course Herbert knows that you must
know: you are not babies.   It is Lizzie Hampson, the dressmaker, who has been asked to go and work at the Elms."

"Oh!" said the rector.   He showed himself wonderfully reasonable,—more reasonable than any one could
have expected.   " I wouldn't let her go there if I was you.
It's not a fit place for a girl."

"We are perfectly well aware of that," said Mrs. Wilber-force. "I warned you from the beginning. But the thing is, who is to prevent her from going? Minnie has told her plainly, it appears, and I will speak to her, and as her clergyman I should say it was your duty to say a word; but whether we shall succeed, that is a different matter. These creatures seem to have a sort of real attraction for everything that is wrong."

"We all have that, I'm afraid, my dear."

"But not all in that way. There may be a bias, but it doesn't take the same form. Do sit down, girls, and take your tea, like reasonable creatures. She shall never enter the rectory, of course, if—and if you are sure Mrs. War-render will do the same. But you know she is very indul-gent,—more indulgent than I should be in her place. There was that story, you know, about Fanny, the laundry-maid. I don't think we shall do much if your dear mother relents, and says the girl is penitent as soon as she cries. She ought to know girls better than that. A little thing makes them cry : but penitence,—that is getting rarer and rarer every day."

"There would be no need for penitence in this case. The girl is a very respectable girl. Don't let her go there, that's all : and give me a cup of tea."

"Isn't that like a man!" said Mrs. Wilberforce. "Don't

let her go there, and give him a cup of tea !—the one just as easy as the other. I am sure I tell you often enough, Herbert, what with all that is done for them and said about them, the poor people are getting more and more unmanageable every day."

"Our family has always been Liberal," said Minnie. " I think the poor people have their rights just as we have. They ought to be educated, and all that."

"Very well," said the other lady; "when you have educated them up to thinking themselves as good—oh, what am I saying? far better—than their betters, you'll see what will come of it. I for one am quite prepared. I pity the people who deceive themselves. Herbert chooses to laugh, but I can't laugh ; it is much too serious for that."

"There will be peace in our days," said the rector ; "and after all, Fanny, we can't have a revolution coming because Lizzie Hampson——"

"Lizzie Hampson," said his wife solemnly, "is a sign of the times. She may be nothing in herself,—none of them are anything in themselves,—but I call her a sign of the times."

"What a grand name for a little girl !" he said, with a laugh. But he added seriously, "I wish that house belonged to Theo, or some one we could bring influence to bear upon ; but what does a city man care ? I wish we could do as the Americans do, and put rollers under it, and cart it away out of the parish."

"Can the Americans do that?"

"They say so. They can do every sort of wonderful thing, I believe."

"And that is what we are coming to!" said Mrs. Wilberforce, with an air of indignant severity, as if this had been the most dreadful accusation in the world.

"I suppose," said the rector, strolling with the young ladies to the gate, "that Theo holds by the family politics? I wonder whether he has given any attention to public questions. At his age a young fellow either does—or he does not," he added, with a laugh. "Oxford often makes a change."

"We don't approve of ladies taking any part in politics," said Minnie, "and I am sure I have never mentioned the subject to Theo."

"But you know, Minnie, mamma said that Theo was—well, I don't remember what she said he was, but certainly not the same as he was brought up."

"Then let us hope he has become a Conservative. Landholders should be and clergy must," said the rector, with a sigh. Then he remembered that this was not a style of conversation likely to commend itself to the two girls. "I hope we shall see you back next Sunday at the Sunday school," he said. "Of course I would not hurry you, if you found it too much; but a little work in moderation I have always thought was the very best thing for a grief like yours. Dear Mrs. Warrender, too," he added softly. He had not been in the habit of calling her dear Mrs. Warrender; but it seemed a term that was appropriate where there had been a death. "I hope she does not quite shut herself up."

"Mamma has been with Lady Markland several times," said Minnie, with a mixture of disapproval and satisfaction. "Naturally, we have been so much thrown together since——"

"To be sure. What a sad thing!—twice in one house, within a week, was it not, the two deaths?"

"Just a week," said Chatty, who loved to be exact.

"But you know Lord Markland was no relation," added Minnie, too conscientious to take to herself the credit of a grief which was not hers. "It was not as if we felt it in that way."

"It was a dreadful thing to happen in one's house, all the same. And Theo, I hear, goes a great deal to Markland. Oh, it is quite natural. He had so much to do for her from the first. And I hear she is a very attractive sort of woman, though I don't know much of her, for my own part."

"Attractive? Well, perhaps she may be attractive, to some people," said Minnie; "but when a woman has been married so long as she has, one never thinks—and her attractiveness has nothing to do with Theo," she added, with some severity.

"Oh no, I suppose not," said the rector. "Tell him I hope we shall soon see him here, for I expect his friend Dick Cavendish in the end of the week. You remember Cavendish? He told me he had met you at Oxford."

"Oh yes," said Chatty quickly. Minnie, who was not accustomed to be forestalled in speech, trod upon this little exclamation, as it were, and spoilt its effect. "Cavendish! I am not sure. I think I do recollect the name," she said.

And then they shook hands with the rector across the gate, and went upon their way. But it was not for the first moment quite a peaceful way. "You were dreadfully ready to say you remembered Mr. Cavendish," said the elder sister. "What do you know of Mr. Cavendish? If I were you, I would not speak so fast, as if Mr. Cavendish were of such importance."

"Oh no, he is of no importance: only I do recollect him quite well. He gave us tea. He was very——"

"He was exactly like other young men," said Miss Warrender. And then they proceeded in silence, Chatty having no desire to contest the statement. She did not

know very much about young men. Their way lay across
the end of the village street, beyond which the trees of the
Warren overshadowed everything. There was only a fence
on that side of the grounds, and to look through it was like
looking into the outskirts of a forest. The rabbits ran
about by hundreds among the roots of the trees. The
birds sang as if in their own kingdom and secure possessions.
To this gentle savagery and dominion of nature the Miss
Warrenders were accustomed; and in the freshness of the
early summer it was sweet. They went on without speaking, for some time, and then it seemed wise to the younger
sister to forestall further remark by the introduction of a
new subject, which, however, was not a usual proceeding
on Chatty's part.

"Minnie," she said, "do you know what the rector
meant when he spoke of Lady Markland, that she was an
attractive woman? You took him up rather sharply."

"No, I didn't," said Minnie, with that ease which is
noticed among near relations. "I said she was rather old
for that."

"She is scarcely any older than you. I know that from
the Peerage. I looked her up."

"So did I," said Miss Warrender. "That does not
make her a day younger or more attractive. She is four
years older than Theo : therefore she is as if she were not

to him. Four years is a dreadful difference when it is on the wrong side."

Chatty was ridiculously simple for a person of three-and-twenty. She said, "I cannot think what that has to do with it. The rector is really very silly at times in what he says."

"I don't see that he is silly. What he means is that Lady Markland will take advantage of Theo, and he will fall in love with her. I should say, for my part, that it is very likely. I have seen a great many things of the kind, though you never open your eyes. He is always going to Markland to see what he can do, if there is anything she wants. He is almost sure to fall in love with her."

"Minnie, a married woman!"

"Oh, you little simpleton! She is not a married woman, she is a widow; and she is left extremely well off and with everything in her hands,—that is to say, she would be very well off if there was any money. A widow is in the best position of any woman. She can do what she likes, and nobody has any right to object."

"Oh, Minnie!" protested the younger sister again.

"You can ask mamma, if you don't believe me. But of course she would not have anything to say to Theo," Miss Warrender said.

CHAPTER XI

"When is Dick Cavendish coming?" said Mrs. Wilberforce to her husband. "I wish he hadn't chosen to come now, of all times in the world, just when we can do nothing to amuse him ; for with the Warrenders in such deep mourning, and those other horrible people on the other side, and things in general getting worse and worse every day——"

"He is not acquainted with the parish, and he does not know that things are getting worse and worse every day. It is a pity about the mourning ; but do you think it is so deep that a game of croquet would be impossible ? Croquet is not a riotous game."

"Herbert !" cried Mrs. Wilberforce. She added in a tone of indignant disapproval, "If you feel equal to suggesting such a thing to girls whose father has not yet been six weeks in his grave, I don't."

The rector was reduced to silence. He was aware that the laws of decorum are in most cases better understood by ladies than by men, and also that the girls at the Warren

would sooner die than do anything that was not according
to the proper rule that regulated the conduct of persons in
their present circumstances. He withdrew, accordingly, to
his study, with rather an uneasy feeling about the visit of
Dick Cavendish. The rector's study was on the opposite
side of the hall, at the end of a short passage, which was a
special providence; for nothing that Mrs. Wilberforce
could do would prevent him from smoking, and by this
means the hall, at least, and the chief sitting-room were
kept free of any suggestions of smoke. He said of himself
that he was not such a great smoker, but there was no
doubt that it was one of the crosses which his wife said
everybody had to bear. That was her cross, her husband's
pipe, and she tried to put up with it like a Christian.
This is one of the cases in which there is very often a conflict of evidence without anything that could be called
perjury on either side: for Mrs. Wilberforce declared to
her confidants (she would not have acknowledged it to the
public for worlds) that her husband smoked morning, noon,
and night; whereas he, when the question was put to him
casually, asserted that he was not at all a great smoker,
though he liked a pipe when he was working, and a cigar
after dinner. "When you are working! Then what a
diligent life you must lead, for I think you are always
working," the wife would remark. "Most of my time,

certainly, dear," said the triumphant husband. There are never very serious jars in a family where smoke takes so important a place. Mr. Wilberforce retired now, and took a pipe to help him to consider. The study was a commodious room, with a line of chairs against the further wall, which the parish mostly took when the bumpkins had anything to say to the parson. A large writing-table, fitted with capacious drawers, stood in the middle of the room, of which one side was for parish business, the other magisterial : for the rector of Underwood was also a justice of the peace, and very active in that respect. He was a man who did not fail in his duty in any way. His sermons he kept in a handsome old carved-oak bureau against the wall, where—for he had been a dozen years in Underwood, and had worked through all the fasts and feasts a great many times—he had executed a classification, and knew where to put his hand on the Christmas sermons, and those for the saints' days, and even for exceptional occasions, such as funerals, almost in the dark. Two large windows, one of which opened upon the lawn, and the other, round the corner, in the other wall of the house, commanded a pretty view of the village, lying with its red roofs in the midst of a luxuriant greenness. Saint Mary-under-wood was the true name of the parish, for it lay in a part of the country which was very rich in trees.

Here he sat down with his friend's letter, and thought. The Cavendishes had once held an important position in the county, and lived in one of the greatest "places" in the neighbourhood. But they had met with a fate not unknown to the greatest favourites, and had descended from their greatness to mediocrity, without, however, sacrificing everything, and indeed with so good a margin that, though they were no longer included among the most eminent gentry of England, they still held the place of a county family. They had shifted their headquarters to a much smaller house, but it was one which had already been possessed by them before they became great. The younger sons, however, had very little to look to, and Dick, who was considered clever, was going to the bar. He was a friend, more or less, of young Warrender's, and had been at Oxford with him, where he was junior to Theo in the university, though his senior in years. For Dick had been a little erratic in his ways. He had not been so orderly and law-abiding as a young English gentleman generally is. He had gone away from home very young, and spent several years in wandering before he would address himself to serious life. He had been in Canada and in the back-woods, and though California was not known then as now, had spent a few months at the gold diggings, in the rude life and strife which English families, not yet acquainted with farming in Manitoba and ranches in the far West, heard of with horror, and where only those sons who were "wild," or otherwise unmanageable, had as yet begun to go. When he returned, and announced that he was going to Oxford, and after that to the bar, it was like the vision of the madman clothed and in his right mind to his parents. This their son who had been lost was found. He came into a little fortune, left him by his godfather, when he returned; and, contrary to the general habit of families in respect to younger sons, his parents were of opinion that if some "nice girl" could be found for Dick it would be the best thing that could happen,—a thing which would lighten their own responsibilities, and probably confirm him in well-doing.

But with all the new-fashioned talk about education and work for women, which then had just begun, nice girls were not quite so sure as they used to be that to reclaim a prodigal, or consolidate a penitence, was their mission in life. Perhaps they were right; but the old idea was good for the race, if not for the individual woman, human sacrifices being a fundamental principle of natural religion, if not of the established creed. And it cannot be said that it was altogether without a thought of finding the appropriate victim that the prodigal had been invited to Underwood. He was not altogether a prodigal, nor would

she be altogether a victim. People do not use such hard
words. He was a young fellow who wanted steadying, for
whom married life (when he had taken his degree), or even
an engagement, might be expected to do much. And the
Miss Warrenders were "nice girls," whose influence might
be of the greatest advantage to him. What need to say
any more?

But it was tiresome that, after having made up this
innocent little scheme for throwing them together, Dick
should choose, of all times in the world, to arrive at the
rectory just after Mr. Warrender's death, when the family
were in mourning, and not "equal to" playing croquet, or
any other reasonable amusement. It was hard, the rector
thought. It was he, and not his wife, strangely enough,
who had thrown himself into this project of match-making.
The Warrender girls were the most well-regulated girls in
the world, and the most likely to keep their respective
husbands straight; and Mr. Wilberforce also thought it
would be a very good thing for the girls themselves, who
were so much out of the way of seeing eligible persons, or
being sought. The rector felt that if Minnie Warrender once
took the young man in hand he was safe. And they had
already met at Oxford during Commemoration, and young
Cavendish had remembered with pleasure their fresh faces
and slightly, pleasantly rustic and old-fashioned ways. He

was very willing to come when he was told that the Wilberforces saw a great deal of Warrender's nice sisters. " Why,
I am in love with them both ! Of course I shall come," he
had said, with his boyish levity. But with equal levity had
put it off from time to time, and at last had chosen the
moment which was least convenient, the most uncomfortable for all parties,—a moment when there was nothing but
croquet, or picnics, or other gentle pleasures which require
feminine co-operation, to amuse the stranger, and when the
feminine co-operation which had been hoped for was for the
time altogether laid on the shelf and out of the question.
Few things could be more trying than this state of
affairs.

Notwithstanding which Dick Cavendish arrived, as had
been arranged. There was nothing remarkable about his
appearance. He was an ordinary brown-haired, blue-eyed
young man,—not, perhaps, ordinary, for that combination
is rather rare,—and there were some people who said that
something in his eye betrayed what they called insincerity ;
indeed there was generally about him an agreeableness,
a ready self-adaptation to everybody's way of thinking, a
desire to recommend himself, which is always open to
censure. Mrs. Wilberforce was one of the people who
shook her head and declared him to be insincere. And as
he went so far as to agree that the empire very possibly was

dropping to pieces, and the education of the poor tending to their and our destruction, in order to please her, it is possible that she was not far wrong. As a matter of fact, however, his tactics were successful even with her; and though she did not relinquish her deep-seated conviction, yet the young man succeeded in flattering and pleasing her, which was all that he wanted, and not that she should vouch for his sincerity. He was very sorry to hear that the Warrenders were in mourning. "I saw the death in the papers," he said, "and thought for a moment that I had perhaps better write and put off; for some people look their worst in mourning. But then I reflected that some others look their best; and their hearts are soft, and a little judicious consolation nicely administered——"

Though it was not perhaps of a very high quality, the rector was delighted with his young friend's wit.

"It must be nicely administered," he said, "and you will not find them inaccessible. They are the best girls in the world, but too natural to make a fuss, as some girls do. He was a very insignificant, neutral-tinted kind of man. I cannot think why they should be supposed to be so inconsolable."

"Oh, Herbert!" said his wife.

"Yes, I know, my dear; but Oh, Herbert, is no argument. Nobody is missed so much as we expect, not the

very best. Life may have to make itself a new channel,
but it flows always on. And when the man is quite insignificant, like poor Mr. Warrender——"

"Don't blaspheme the dead, Herbert. It is dreadful
to hear you, you are so cynical; and when even a clergyman takes up such opinions, what can we expect of other
people?" Mrs. Wilberforce said, with marked disapproval,
as she left the gentlemen after dinner. She left them in a
novel sort of way, going out of the window of the dining-
room to the lawn, which ran along all that side of the
house. The drawing-room, too, opened upon it, and one
window of the rector's study; and the line of limes, very
fine trees, which stood at a little distance, throwing a
delightful shadow with their great silken mass of foliage
over the velvety grass, made the lawn into a kind of great
withdrawing-room, spacious and sweet. Mrs. Wilberforce
had a little settlement at one end of this, with wicker-work
chairs and a table for her work and one for tea, while her
husband, at the other end, clinging to his own window,
which provided a mode of escape in case any one should
appear to whom his cigar might be offensive, smoked at the
other, throwing now and then a few words at her between
the puffs. While thus indulging himself he was never
allowed to approach more near.

"I am afraid we have not very much amusement for

you," the rector said. "There is nothing going on at this season, and the Warren, as my wife says, is shut up."

"Not so much shut up but that one may go to see Warrender?"

"Oh no."

"And in that case the ladies must be visible, too : for I entertained them, you know, in my rooms at Commem. They must at least ask me to tea. They owe me tea."

"Well, if you are content with that. My wife is dreadfully particular, you know. I daresay we may be able to manage a game, for all Mrs. Wilberforce says; and if the worst comes to the worst, Dick, I suppose you can exist without the society of ladies for a few days."

"So long as I have Mrs. Wilberforce to fall back upon, and Flo. Flo is growing very pretty, perhaps you don't know? Parents are so dull to that sort of thing. But there is somebody else in the parish I have got to look after. What is their name? I can't recollect, but I know the name of the house. It is the Elms."

"The Elms, my dear fellow!" cried the rector, with consternation. He turned pale with fright and horror, and, rising, went softly and closed the window, which his wife had left open. "For Heaven's sake," he said, "don't speak so loud ; my wife might hear."

"Why shouldn't she hear?" said Dick undaunted.

" There's nothing wrong, is there? I don't remember the people's name——"

" No, most likely not; one name will do as well as another," said the rector solemnly. " Dick, I know that a young fellow like you looks at things in another light from a man of my cloth; but there are things that can be done, and things that can't, and it is simply impossible, you know, that you should visit at a place like that from my house."

" What do you mean by a place like that? I know nothing about the place. It belongs to my uncle Cornwall, and there is something to be done to it, or they won't stay."

The rector drew a long breath. " You relieve me very much," he said. " Is the Mr. Cornwall that bought the Elms your uncle Cornwall—without a joke? Then you must tell him, Dick, there's a good fellow, to do nothing to it, but for the love of Heaven help us to get those people away."

" Who are the people?" said the astonished Dick. It is uncertain whether Mr. Wilberforce managed to make any articulate reply, but he sputtered forth some broken words, which, with the look that accompanied them, gave to his visitor an idea of the fact which had been for a month or two whispered, with bated breath, by the villagers and people about. Dick, who was still nominally of the faction of the reprobates, fell a-laughing when the news penetrated his mind. It was not that his sympathies were with vice as against virtue, as the rector was disposed to believe ; but the thought of the righteous and strait-laced uncle, who had sent him into what would have been to Mr. Cornwall the very jaws of hell, and of all that might have happened had he himself, Dick, announced in Mrs. Wilberforce's presence his commission to the Elms, was too comical to be resisted, and the peals of his laughter reached the lady on the lawn, and brought the children pressing to the dining-room window to see what had happened. Flo, of whom Dick had said that she was getting pretty, but who certainly was not shy, and had no fear of finding herself out of place, came pertly and tapped at the window, and, looking in with her little sunny face, demanded to know what was the fun, so that Dick burst forth again and again. The rector did not see the fun, for his part; he saw no fun at all. Even when Dick, almost weeping with the goodness of the joke, endeavoured to explain how droll it was to think of his old uncle sending him there, Mr. Wilberforce did not see it. "My wife will ask me what you were laughing about, and how am I to tell her? She will see no joke in it, and she will not believe that I was not laughing with you—at all that is most sacred, Emily will say." No one who had seen the excellent rector at that moment would have accused him of sharing in the laughter, for his face was as blankly serious as if he had been at a funeral: but he knew the view which Mrs. Wilberforce was apt to take.

And his fears came so far true that he did undergo a rigid cross-questioning as soon as the guest was out of the way. And though the rector was as discreet as possible, it yet became deeply impressed upon the mind of his wife that the fun had something to do with the Elms. That gentlemen did joke on such subjects, which were not fit to be talked about, she was fully aware; but that her own husband, a man privileged beyond most men, a clergyman of the Church of England, should do it, was bitter indeed to her. "I know what young men are," she said; "they are all the same. I know there is nothing that amuses and attracts them so much as improper people. But, Herbert, you! and when vice is at our very doors, to laugh! Oh, don't say another word to me on the subject!" Mrs. Wilberforce cried.

CHAPTER XII.

The recollection of that unexplained and ill-timed merriment clouded over the household horizon even next morning; but Dick was so cheerful and so much at his ease that things ameliorated imperceptibly. The heart of a woman, even when most disapproving, is softened by the man who takes the trouble to make himself agreeable to her children. She thought that there could not be so very much harm in him, after all, when she saw the little ones clustering about him, one on his knees and one on his shoulders. "There is a sort of instinct in children," she said afterwards: and most people would be in this respect of Mrs. Wilberforce's opinion. And about noon the rector took his guest to call at the Warren. Though this was not what an ordinary stranger would have been justified in doing, yet when you consider that he had known Theo at Oxford and entertained the ladies at Commem., you will understand why the rector took this liberty. "I suppose I may ask the girls and Theo to come over in the afternoon," said Mr. Wilberforce.

"Oh, certainly, Herbert, you may *ask* them," she replied, but with a feeling that if Minnie accepted it would be as if the pillars of the earth were shaken ; though indeed in the circumstances with a young man on her hands to be amused for all the lingering afternoon, Mrs. Wilberforce herself would have been very willing that they should come Dick Cavendish was a pleasant companion for a morning walk.   He admired the country in its fresh greenness, as they went along, though its beauty was not striking.   He admired the red village, clustering under the warmth and fulness of the foliage, and pleased the rector, who naturally felt his own *amour propre* concerned in the impression made by his parish upon a new spectator.   "We must come to old England for this sort of thing," said Dick, looking back upon the soft rural scene with the half-patronising experience of a man *qui en a vu bien d'autres.*   And the rector was pleased, especially as it was not all undiscriminating praise.   When they got within the grounds of the Warren criticism came in.   "What does Warrender mean," Dick said, "by letting everything run up in this wild way ? the trees have no room to breathe."

"You must recollect that Theo has just come into it. And the old gentleman was long feeble, and very conservative,—though not in politics, as I could have wished."

"Ah, I thought Warrender was a bit of a radical : but

they say a man always becomes more or less a Tory when he comes into his property. I have no experience," said Dick, with his light-hearted laugh. Had Mrs. Wilberforce heard him, she would have found in it that absence of respect for circumstances which she considered to be one of the signs of the times ; and it had a startling and jarring effect upon the individual who did hear it, who was disturbed by it in the stillness of his morning walk and thoughts. It broke the silence of the brooding air, and awakened impertinent echoes everywhere, Nature being always glad of the opportunity. The young owner of the place was himself absorbed in a warm haze of visions, like his own trees in the hush of the noon. Any intrusion was disagreeable to him. Nevertheless, when he saw the rector he came forward with that consciousness of the necessity of looking pleased which is one of the vexations of a recluse. What did he mean by bringing men here, where nobody wanted either them or him ? But when he saw who it was who accompanied the rector, Warrender's face and the line of annoyance in his forehead softened a little ; for Dick was one of the men who are everywhere welcome. Warrender even smiled as he held out his hand.

"You, Cavendish ! Who could have thought of seeing you here ?"

"I am afraid I am rather presuming : but I could not

be so near without coming to see you." Dick grew grave,
as was incumbent in the circumstances, and though he had
no doubt whatever of seeing the ladies added a sort of
humble suggestion : " I am afraid I can scarcely hope to
pay my respects ?"

" You must come in and see my mother," Warrender
said.

The house, as has been said, looked its best when
shade and coolness were a necessity of the season ; but the
visitor who came with keen eyes, observing everything, not
because he had any special object, but because he could
not help it, took in in a moment the faded air of solid
respectability, the shabbiness which does not mean poverty,
the decent neglect, as of a place whose inhabitants took no
hought of such small matters, which showed everywhere.
It was not neglect, in the ordinary sense of the word, for
all was carefully and nicely arranged, fresh flowers on the
tables, and signs of living—but rather a composed and
decorous content. The girls, as they were always called,
were found, Chatty with her hands full of flowers and a
number of china vases before her, standing at an old
buffet in the hall, and Minnie just coming out of the dining-
room, where she had been doing her morning needle-work,
which was of a plain and homely description, not calculated
to be seen by visitors. The old buffet in the hall was not

like the mahogany catafalque in the other rooms, and the flowers were very fresh and the china of unappreciated antiquity. Perhaps these accessories helped to make the modest little picture of Charlotte arranging the flowers a pretty one; and she was young and fresh and modest and unconscious; her figure was pretty and light; her look, as she raised her head and blushed to see the little party of men, so guileless, frank, and good that, though the others, who were used to her, thought nothing of her, to Dick it appeared that Chatty was a very pleasant thing to see against the dim background of the old respectable house.

"It is Mr. Cavendish," said Minnie. "How curious! It is true sometimes, no doubt, as everybody says, that talk of an angel and you see its wings; but generally it is just the person whom one least thinks of who appears."

"That is very hard upon me," said Dick. "My mind has been so full of you for twenty-four hours that you ought to have thought a little upon me, if only on the theory of brain waves."

"I hope you don't believe in anything of that sort. How should you think of people when there is nothing to put you in mind of them? If we had been in Oxford, indeed — Come into the drawing-room; we shall find mamma there. And how is dear Mrs. Wilberforce?"

"She wants you all," said the rector, in a low voice aside, "to come over this afternoon to tea."

"To tea, when you have company! Oh, she could not—she never could expect such a thing!"

"Do you call one of your brother's friends company,—one? I should say it took three at least to constitute company. And I want Theo to come. Mind what I say. If you don't amuse him, Theo will think of nothing but going to Markland. He goes to Markland more than I like already."

"Mr. Wilberforce, I am not one that believes in love being blind, and I know all Theo's faults; but to think that he is courting amusement,—amusement, and papa only dead six weeks!"

"I did not say amusement," said the rector crossly. "I said to be amused, which is quite different; not to be left for ever in the same state of mind, not to lie vacant."

"You must have a very poor opinion of him and of all of us," said Miss Warrender, leading the way into the drawing-room, where the others had gone before them. Chatty remained behind, being still busy with her flowers. The rector and Minnie were supposed to be talking parish talk, and to have lingered with that purpose. Chatty thought it sounded too animated to be all about the clothing club and the mothers' meetings, but she supposed that some one must have gone wrong, which was generally the exciting element in parish talk. She was not herself excited by it, being greatly occupied how to make the big white Canterbury bells stand up as they ought in the midst of a large bouquet, in a noble white and blue Nankin vase, which was meant for the table in the hall.

Mrs. Warrender was very glad to see young Cavendish. She asked at once if they were going to take him to Hurst Hill and the old castle at Pierrepoint, and entered almost eagerly into a description of what could be done for a stranger. "For we have scarcely anything, except the country itself, to show a stranger," she said. "There is nothing that is exciting, not much society, and unfortunately, at this moment, the little that there was——"

"I know," said Dick, "it is my misfortune. I was deeply sorry to hear——" He had never seen Mr. Warrender, and naturally could have no profound regret on the subject, but his eyes expressed so much tender sympathy that her heart was touched, and tears came to her own.

"You are very kind to take a part in our sorrows," she said. "If all had been well with us, there would have been no one more pleased than he to make our country pleasant to you. He was always so much interested in Theo's friends. But even as things are, if you do not find it too sad, we shall always be glad to see you. Not that we have anything to tempt you," she added, with a smile.

"Then, Mrs. Warrender," said the rector, "may I tell my wife that you are not going away?"

Mrs. Warrender cast a wistful look round her,—at her son, at the remorseless inclosure of those dull walls, which were like those of a prison. "It appears not, for the present," she said.

"No," said Minnie; "for where can we be so well as at home? For my part, I don't believe in change. What do you change? Only the things about you. You can't change yourself nor your circumstances."

"The skies, but not the soul," said Dick.

"That is just what I mean, Mr. Cavendish. I see you understand. Mamma thinks it would be more cheerful to go away. But we don't really want to be cheerful. Why should we be cheerful?—at least for six months, or I should say a year. We can't be supposed to be equal to anything, after our great loss, in less than a year."

At this they were all silent, a little overawed; and then Mrs. Warrender returned to her original discourse upon Pierrepoint Castle and the Hurst at Cleveland: "They are both excellent places for picnics. You should take Mr. Cavendish there."

"That was all very well," said the rector, "when there

was all of you to fall back upon ; but he must be content
with the domestic croquet and the mild gratification of
walks, in present circumstances.   Has Theo come to any
decision about the improvements ?   I suppose you will not
begin to cut down till the autumn ?"

"Everything is at a standstill, Mr. Wilberforce."

"Well," said Theo, almost angrily, turning to the
rector, "there is no hurry, I hope.   One need not start,
axe in hand, as if one had been waiting for that.   There
is time enough, in autumn or in spring, or when it happens
to be convenient.   I am in no haste, for my part."

There was again a little pause, for there had been
temper in Theo's tones.   And then it was that the rector
distinguished himself by the most ill-timed question,—a
question which startled even Chatty, who was coming in
at the moment with a bowl full of roses, carried in both
hands.   Yet it was a very innocent-seeming question, and
Cavendish was not aware of any significance in it till he
saw the effect it produced.   "How," said Mr. Wilberforce
very distinctly, "is Lady Markland ?"   He was looking
straight at Theo, but as the words came out of his
mouth, struck too late by their inappropriateness, turned
and looked Mrs. Warrender somewhat severely in the face.

"Oh !" she said, as if some one had struck her ; and
as for Warrender, he sprang to his feet, and walked across

the room to one of the windows, where he stood pulling to
pieces one of Chatty's bouquets.   She put down her roses,
and stood with her hands dropped and her mouth a little
open, a picture of innocent consternation, which, however,
was caused more by the effect upon the others than by any
clear perception in herself.   All this took place in a
moment, and then Mrs. Warrender replied sedately, " The
last time I saw her she was well enough in health.   Sor—
trouble," she added, changing the word, " does not always
affect the health."

" And does she mean to stay *there ?*" the rector said,
feeling it necessary to follow up his first question.   Mrs.
Warrender hesitated, and began to reply that she did not
know, that she believed nothing was settled, that—when
Theodore suddenly turned and replied :—

" Why shouldn't she stay?   The reason is just the
same for her as for us.   Death changes little except to
the person immediately concerned.   It is her home : why
shouldn't she stay?"

" Really," said the rector, " you take it so seriously I—
when you put the question to me, I——   As a matter of
fact," he added, " I did not mean anything, if I must tell
the truth.   I just said the first thing that occurred.   And
a change is always the thing that is first thought of after
such a—after such a——"   The rector sought about for

a word. He could not say calamity, or affliction, or any of the words that are usually employed. He said at last, with a sense of having got triumphantly over the difficulty —"such a shock."

"I agree with the rector," said Minnie. "It would be far better that she should go away, for a change. The circumstances are quite different. For a lady to go and look after everything herself, when it ought not to be supposed possible that she could do anything: seeing the lawyers, and giving the orders, and acting exactly as if nothing had happened,—oh, it is too dreadful! It is quite different from us. And she does not even wear a widow's cap! That would be reason enough for going away, if there was nothing else. She ought to go away for the first year, not to let anybody know that she has never worn a widow's cap."

"Now that is a very clever reason," said Dick Cavendish, who felt it was time for him to interfere, and lessen the serious character of the discussion. "Unaided, I should never have thought of that. Do at Rome as Rome does; or if you don't, go out of Rome, and don't expose yourself. There is a whole system of social philosophy in it."

"Oh, I am not a philosopher," cried Minnie, "but I know what I think. I know what my opinion is."

"We are not here to criticise Lady Markland," said

her mother ; and then she burst into an unpremeditated invitation, to break the spell. " You will bring Mr. Cavendish to dine with us one evening?" she said. " He and you will excuse the dulness of a sad house."

The rector felt his breath taken from him, and thought of what his wife would say. " If you are sure it will not be too much for you," he replied.

Dick's eyes and attention were fixed upon the girls. Minnie's face expressed the utmost horror. She opened her mouth to speak ; her sharp eyes darted dagger thrusts at her mother ; it was evident that she was bursting with remonstrance and denunciation. Chatty, on the contrary, looked at her mother, and then at the stranger, with a soft look of pleasure stealing over her face. It softened still more the rounded outline, the rose tints, which were those of a girl of seventeen rather than twenty-three, and which her black dress brought out with double force. Dick thought her quite pretty,—nay, very pretty,—as she stood there, her sleeves thrust a little back on her arms,— her hands a little wet with the flowers, her face owning a half guilty pleasure of which she was half ashamed. The others were involved in thoughts quite different : but innocent Chatty. relieved by the slightest lifting of the cloud, and glad that somebody should be coming to dinner, was to him the central interest of the group.

"You put your foot in it, I think," he said to the rector, as they walked back, "but I could not quite make out how. Who is the unhappy woman, lost to all sense of shame, who wears no widow's cap?"

"I meant no harm," said the rector. "It was quite natural that I should ask for Lady Markland. Of course it stands to reason that as he died there, and they were mixed up with the whole business, and she is not in my parish, they should know more of her than I."

"And so old Warrender is mixed up with a beautiful widow," said Dick. "He doesn't seem the sort of fellow: but I suppose something of that sort comes to most men, one time or another," he added, with a half laugh.

"What, a widow?" said the rector, with a smile. "Eh? What are you saying? What is that? Well, as you ask, that is the Elms, Cavendish, where I suppose you no longer have any desire to go."

"Oh, that is the Elms, is it?" said Cavendish. His voice had not its usual cheerful sound. He stood quite still, with an interest which the rector thought quite uncalled for. The Elms was a red brick house, tall like the rectory, and of a similar date, the upper stories of which appeared over a high wall. The quick shutting of a door in this wall was the thing which had awakened the interest of Cavendish. A girl had come hurriedly, furtively, out, and with the apparent intention of closing it noiselessly had let the door escape from her hand, and marked her departure by a clang which for a moment filled the air. She glanced round her hastily, and with a face in which a very singular succession of emotions were painted looked in the faces of the gentlemen. The first whom she noticed was evidently the rector, to whom she gave a glance of terror : but then turned to Dick, with a look of amazement which seemed to take every other feeling away,—amazement and recognition. She stared at him for a moment as if paralysed, and then, fluttering like a bird in her light dress, under the high, dark line of the wall, hurried away.

" Bless me," said the rector troubled, " Lizzie Hampson! Now I recollect that was what the ladies were saying. Silly girl, she has gone, after all ; but I must put a stop to that. How she stared at you, Dick, to be sure !"

" Yes, she has got a sharp pair of eyes. I think she will know me again," said Dick, with what seemed to the rector rather forced gaiety. " Rather a pretty little girl, all the same. What did you call her? Is she one of your parishioners? She looked mighty frightened of you."

" Lizzie Hampson," said the rector. " She is the granddaughter of the old woman at the shop. She is half a foreigner I believe : but I always thought—Bless me !

Emily will be very sorry, but very angry too, I am afraid. I wish I had not seen it. I wish we had not come this way."

" Do you think you are obliged to tell? It was only by accident that we saw her," said Cavendish. " It would hurt nobody if you kept it to yourself."

" I daresay the poor little thing meant no harm," said the rector to himself; "it is natural to want to make a little more money. I am entering into temptation, but I cannot help it. Do you think, after all, I might say nothing about seeing her? We should not have seen her, you know, if we had come home the other way."

"Give her the benefit of the possibility," said Dick, with a short laugh. But he seemed to be affected too, which was wonderfully sympathetic and nice of him, with what troubled the rector so much. He scarcely talked at all for the rest of the way. And though he was perhaps as gay as ever at lunch, there came over him from time to time a curious abstraction, quite out of character with Dick Cavendish. In the afternoon, Warrender and Chatty came in, as they had been invited to tea (not Minnie, which satisfied Mrs. Wilberforce's sense of right), and a very quiet game of croquet, a sort of whisper of a game, under their breath, as it were, was played. And in this way the day passed. The visitor declared in the evening that he had enjoyed himself immensely. But he had a headache, and instead of coming in to prayers went out in the dark for a walk ; which was not at all the sort of thing which Mrs. Wilberforce liked her visitors to do.

CHAPTER XIII

DICK CAVENDISH went out for a walk. It was a little chilly after the beautiful day; there was rain in the air, and neither moon nor stars, which in the country, where there are no means of artificial lighting, makes it unpleasant for walking. He went right into the big clump of laurels, and speared himself on the prickles of the old hawthorn before he emerged from the Rectory gates. After that it was easier. Many of the cottage people were indeed going to bed, but by the light which remained in a window here and there he was able to preserve himself from accident as he strolled along. Two or three dogs, sworn enemies to innovation, scented him, and protested at their loudest against the novelty, not to say wickedness, of a passenger at that hour of the night. It was, perhaps, to them what Lizzie Hampson's independence was to Mrs. Wilberforce,— a sign of the times. He made his way along, stumbling here and there, sending into the still air the odour of his cigar, towards the spot where the window of the little shop shone in the distance like a low, dim, somewhat smoky star, the rays of which shaped themselves slightly iridescent against the thick damp atmosphere of the night. Cavendish went up to this dull shining, and stared through the window for a moment through the sticks of barley sugar and boxes of mustard and biscuits. He did not know there was any special significance in the sight of Lizzie Hampson seated there within the counter, demurely sewing, and apparently unconscious of any spectators, but it was enough to have startled any of the neighbours who were aware of Lizzie's ways. The old grandmother had gone to see her daughter in the village, who was ill ; but in such cases it was Lizzie's way to leave the door of the room in which she sat open, and to give a very contemptuous attention to the tinkle of the little bell attached to the door which announced a customer. Now, however, she sat in the shop, ready to supply anything that might be wanted. Dick strolled past quietly, and went a little way on beyond, but then he came back. He did not linger at the window, as one of Lizzie's admirers might have done. He passed it twice ; then, with a somewhat anxious gaze round him, went in. He asked for matches, with a glance at the open door of the room behind. Lizzie said nothing, but something in her look gave him as well as words could have done an assurance of safety. He had closed the door of the shop behind him. He now said quickly, "Then I was not mistaken, and it is you, Lizzie."

There was not the slightest appearance in her of the air of a rustic flirt waiting for a lover, still less of anything more objectionable. Her look was serious, full of resistance and even of defiance, as if the encounter was against her will, though it was necessary that it should be. "Yes, sir," she said shortly, "you were not mistaken, and it is me."

"And what are you doing here?"

"Nothing that isn't right," said Lizzie. "I'm living with my grandmother, as any one will tell you, and working at my trade."

"Well—that is all right," he said, after a moment's hesitation.

"I don't suppose that you sought me out just for that, sir—to give me your approbation," the girl said quickly.

"For which you don't care at all," he said, with a half laugh.

"No more than you care for what I'm doing, whether it's good or bad."

"Well," he said, "I suppose so far as that goes we are about even, Lizzie: though I, for one, should be sorry to hear any harm of you. Do you ever hear anything—of your mistress—that was?"

She gave him a keen look. All the time her hands
were busy with a little pile of match-boxes, the pretence
which was to explain his presence had any one appeared.
" She is—living, if that is what you mean," Lizzie said.

" Living ! Oh yes, I suppose so—at her age. Is she
—where she was ?"

Lizzie looked at him, again investigating his face keenly,
and he at her. They were like two antagonists in a duel,
each on his guard, each eagerly observant of every point at
which he could have an advantage. At last, " Where was
that, sir?" she said. " I don't know where you heard of
her last."

Dick made no answer. It was some moments before
he spoke at all. Then, " Is she in England?" he said.

" I'm not at liberty, sir, to say where she is."

" You know, of course. I can see that in your face.
Is she——But perhaps you don't intend to answer any
question I put to you."

" I think not, sir," said Lizzie firmly. " What would
be the good ? She don't want you, nor you——"

" Nor I her : it is true," he said. His face became
very grave, almost stern. " I have little reason to wish to
know. Still you must be aware that misery is the end of
such a way of life."

" Oh, you need give yourself no trouble about that,"

cried Lizzie, with something like scorn; "she is a deal better off and more thought upon than ever she would have been if——"

"Poor girl!" he said. These words and the tone in which they were spoken stopped the quick little angry speech that was on Lizzie's lips. She wavered for a moment, then recovered herself.

"If you please," she said, "to take your matches, sir. It ain't general for gentlemen like you to come into granny's shop: and we think a deal of little things here. It is not as if we were—on the other side."

He laughed with a sort of fierce ridicule that offended the girl. "So—I might be supposed to be coming after you," he said.

She flung the matches to him across the counter. "There may be more difference here than there was *there*: but a gentleman, if he is a gentleman, will be civil wherever he is."

"You are quite right," said Dick, recovering himself, "and I spoke like a fool. For all that you say, misery is the end of such a life; and if I could help it I should not like her to come to want."

"Oh!" said Lizzie, with exasperation, stamping her foot. "Want yourself! You are more like to come to it than she is. I could show you in a moment—I could just

let you see——" Here she paused, and faltered, and grew
red, meeting his eyes. He did not ask any further
questions. He had grown pale as she grew red. Their
looks exchanged a rapid communication, in which neither
Lizzie's reluctance to speak nor his hesitation in asking was
of any avail. He put down the sixpence which he had in
his hand upon the counter, and went out into the night in
a dumb confusion of mind, as if he had received a blow.

Here, breathing the same air, seeing the same sights,
within reach! He went a little further on in the darkness,
not knowing where, nor caring, in the bewilderment of the
shock which had come to him unawares, and suddenly in
the dark was aware of a range of lighted windows which
seemed to hang high in the air—the windows of the Elms
appearing over the high garden wall. He went along
towards the house mechanically, and only stopped when
his shoulder rubbed against the bricks, near the spot where
he had seen Lizzie come out, as he walked past. The
lights moved about from window to window; the house
seemed full of movement and life; and within the wall
there was a sound of conversation and laughter. Did he
recognise the voices, or any one among them? He did not
say so even to himself, but turned round and hurried back,
stumbling through the darkness which hid and blinded him.
In the village he met a woman with a lantern, who he did

not doubt was Lizzie's grandmother, the village authority; no doubt a gossip, quite disposed to search into other people's mysteries, quite unaware of the secret story which had connected itself with his own. She passed him in a little mist of light in the midst of the dark, raising her head instinctively as he passed with a sense of something unfamiliar, but of course not seeing who he was. Presently he found his way again into the Rectory garden, avoiding the prickles of the tree against which he had spiked himself on his way out. Mrs. Wilberforce was on her way upstairs with her candle as he came in. She looked at him disapprovingly, and hoped, with something like irony, that he had enjoyed his walk. " Though you must have had to grope along in the dark, which does not seem much of a pleasure."

" The air is delightful," said Dick, with unnecessary fervour. " I like a stroll in the dark, and the lights in the cottages are pretty to see."

" Dear me, I should have thought everybody was in bed; but late hours are creeping in with other things," said the rector's wife as she went upstairs. The rector himself was standing at the door of his study, with an unlighted pipe in his hand. " Come and have a smoke," he said. For a moment it occurred to Cavendish, though rather as a temptation than as a relief, to tell the story which seemed

to fill his mind like something palpable, leaving room for
nothing else, to his simple-minded rural friend, an older
man than himself and a clergyman, and therefore likely to
have received other confidences before now. But something sealed his lips ; the very atmosphere of the house, the
narrow life with its thousand little occupations, in which
there was an ideal yet prosaic innocence, an incapacity
even to understand those elements of which tragedy is
made. How could he say it—how reveal anything so alien
to every possibility ! He might have told the good Wilberforce had he been in debt or in love, or any light difficulty
in which the parson might have played the part of mediator,
whether with an angry father or an irritated creditor. He
would have made an excellent confidant in such cases, but
not in this.

In debt or in love—in love ! Dick Cavendish's character
was well known ; or so, at least, everybody thought. He
was always in love, just as he was always in good spirits,—a
fellow full of frolic and fun, only too light-hearted to take
life with sufficient seriousness ; and life must be taken
seriously if you are going to make anything of it. This
had been said to him a great many times since he came
home. There was no harm known of him, as there generally is of a young man who lets a few years drop in the hey-
day of life. He liked his fun, the servants said, which was

their way of putting it: and his parents considered that he
did not take life with sufficient seriousness; the two verdicts
were the same. But the people most interested in him had
almost unanimously agreed in that theory, of which mention
has been already made, about the "nice girl." He was
himself aware of the plan and had got a great deal of
amusement out of it. Whether it came to anything else or
not, it at least promised him a great deal of pleasure.
Scores of nice girls had been invited to meet him, and all
his relatives and friends had laid themselves out thus to
make a reformed character of Dick. He liked them all,
he declared; they were delightful company, and he did
not mind how many he was presented to; for what can be
nicer than a nice girl? and to see how many of them there
were in the world was exhilarating to a man fresh out of the
backwoods. As he had never once approached the limits
of the serious, or had occasion to ask himself what might
be the end of any of these pleasant triflings into which his
own temperament, seconding the plots of his friends, carried
him lightly, all had gone quite well and easily, as Dick
loved the things about him to go. But suddenly, on this
occasion, when there was an unexpected break in the
pleasant surface of affairs, and dark remembrances, never
forgotten, had got uppermost in his mind; in this night of
all others, when those two words, "in love," floated through

his mind, there rose up with them a sudden apparition,—
the figure, light, yet not shadowy, of Chatty Warrender
holding the bowl of roses with both hands, and with that
look of innocent surprise and pleasure in her face. Who
can account for such appearances? She walked into his
imagination at the mere passage of these words through his
head, stepping across the threshold of his fancy with almost
as strong a sensation of reality as if she had pushed open
his door and come into the room in which he was to all
appearance quite tranquilly taking off his boots and changing
his coat to join the rector in the study below. He had
seen a great many girls more beautiful, more clever, more
striking in every way, than Chatty. He had not been
aware, even, that he had himself distinguished her; yet
there she was, with her look, which was not addressed to
him, yet perhaps was more or less on account of him,—
that look of unexpected pleasure. Was it on his account?
No; only because in the midst of the dulness some one
was asked to dinner. Bah! he said to himself, and tossed
the boot he had taken off upon the floor—in the noisy way
that young men do before they learn in marriage how to
behave themselves, was the silent comment of Mrs. Wilberforce, who heard him, as she made her preparations for
bed, next door.

Dick was not so jolly as usual, in the hour of smoke

and converse which ensued. It was usually the rector's favourite hour, the moment for expansion, for confidences, for assurances on his part, to his young friends, that life in the company of a nice woman, and with your children growing up round you, was in reality a far better thing than your clubs and theatres—although a momentary regret might occasionally cross the mind, and a strong desire for just so many reasonable neighbours as might form a whist-party. Dick was in the habit of making fun of the rector's self-congratulations and regrets, but on this evening he scarcely made a single joke. Three or four times he relapsed into that silence, meditative or otherwise, which is permitted and even enjoyable in the midst of smoke, when two men are confidential without saying anything, and are the best of company without exchanging one idea. But in the midst of one of those pauses, which was more remarkable, he suddenly sat bolt upright in his chair, and said, "I am afraid I must leave you to-morrow," taking away the rector's breath.

"Leave us to-morrow! Why in the name of wonder should you leave us to-morrow?" Mr. Wilberforce cried.

"Well, the truth is," said Dick, "you see I have been away from home a considerable time : and my people are going abroad very soon ; and then I've been remiss, you know, in my home duties."

"But you knew all that, my dear fellow, yesterday as well as to-day."

"That's true," said Dick, with a laugh. "The fact is that's not all, Wilberforce. I have had letters."

"Letters! Has there been a delivery? Bless my soul!" said the rector, "this is something quite new."

"Look here," said Dick. "I have been out, and I passed by the—the post-office, and there I got news—Come, don't look at me in that violent way. I have got news, and there is an end of it, which makes me think I had better clear out of this."

"If you want to make a mystery, Cavendish," said the rector, slowly knocking out the ashes of his pipe.

"I don't want to make any mystery," said Dick; then he added, "If I did, it would be, of course, because I could not help it. Sometimes a man is mixed up in a mystery which he can't throw any light upon, for—for other people's sake."

"Ah!" said Mr. Wilberforce. He refilled the pipe very deliberately, and with a very grave face. Then, with a sudden flash of illumination, "I make no doubt," he cried, "it's something about those tenants of your uncle's. He is urging you to go to the Elms."

"Well, since you have guessed, that is about it," said Cavendish. "I can't carry out my commission, and as I'd rather not explain to him——"

"Why shouldn't you explain to him? I have quite been calculating that you would explain to him, and get him to take action, and free us of a set of people so much —so entirely," cried the indignant rector, "out of our way!"

"Well, you see," said Dick, "it's not such an easy thing to get people out of a house. I know enough about law to know that; and the old fellow would be in a terrible way if he knew. I don't want to worry him, don't you see? so the best thing I can do is to say I left very soon, and had not the time to call."

"Well, for one thing, I am rather glad to hear you say so," said the rector; "for I thought at first, by the way you introduced the subject, that your uncle himself, who has always borne such an excellent character, was somehow mixed up——"

Cavendish replied by a peal of laughter so violent as almost to look hysterical. He laughed till the tears ran down his cheeks. "Poor old uncle," he said,—"poor old fellow! After a long and blameless life to be suspected, and that by a clergyman!"

"Cavendish," said the rector severely, "you are too bad; you make fun of things the most sacred. It is entirely your fault if I ever associated in my mind for a moment—— However," he added, "there is one thing certain : you can't go away till you have dined at the Warren, according to Mrs. Warrender's invitation. In her circumstances one must be doubly particular, and as she made an effort for Theo's sake, and yours as his friend——"

" Oh, she made an effort ! I did not think of that."

" If you are in such a hurry, Emily can find out in the morning whether to-morrow will suit them, and one day longer will not matter, surely. I can't conceive why you should feel such an extreme delicacy about it."

" Oh, that's my way," said Dick lightly. " I am extremely delicate about everything, though you don't seem to find it out."

" I wish you could be a little serious about something," said the rector, with a sigh. " Things are not all made to get a laugh out, though you seem to think so, Dick."

" It is as good a use as another," said Dick. But as he went upstairs shortly after, the candle which he carried in his hand lighted up, in the midst of the darkness of the peaceful, sleeping house, a face which revealed anything rather than an inclination to get laughter out of everything. Nevertheless, he had pledged himself to stay for the dinner at the Warren which was to cost Mrs. Warrender an effort. It might cost him more than an effort, he said to himself.

CHAPTER XIV

"ONE day is the same to us as another. We see nobody."

"Oh, of course!" said Mrs. Wilberforce. " Dear Mrs. Warrender, it is so noble of you to make such an effort. I hope Theo will appreciate it as it deserves."

Mrs. Warrender coloured a little, as one is apt to do when condemned by too much praise. It is difficult sometimes to tell which is worse, the too little or the too much : but she did not make any reply.

" But I am glad it does not make any difference to have us to-night; that is, if you meant me to come?—or perhaps it was only the two gentlemen? I see now : to be sure, two gentlemen is no party; they need not even come back to the drawing-room at all. I am so glad I came to inquire, for now I understand perfectly. And you are sure it will quite suit you to have them to-night ?"

"Of course," said Minnie, " Mamma does not look upon you as company, dear Mrs. Wilberforce; it will be only a relief if you come, for gentlemen, and especially new people, who don't know what we have lost nor anything about us, are trying. Mr. Cavendish, I remember, was quite nice when we had tea in his rooms at Commemoration, and if all had been well—— But I am sure mamma forms too high an estimate of her own powers. What I am afraid of is that she will break down."

" To be sure, dear Minnie, if you are afraid of that——" said the rector's wife, and so it was settled. Chatty took no part at all in the arrangements. She had not joined in her sister's severe animadversions as to the dinner-party. For herself, she was glad of the change ; it might be wrong, but she could not help being glad. It was, she acknowledged to herself, rather dull never to see any but the same faces day after day. And Mr. Cavendish was very nice ; he had a cheerful face, and such a merry laugh. To be sure, it would not be right for Chatty herself to laugh, in the circumstances, in her deep mourning, but it was a mild and surely innocent gratification to listen to the laugh of another. The Wilberforces were very great friends and very nice, but they always remembered what had happened, and toned themselves—these were the words Mrs. Wilberforce used—toned themselves to the subdued condition of the family. Chatty thought that, however nice (and most thoughtful) that might be, it was pleasant now and then to

be in company with somebody who did not tone himself,
but laughed freely when he had a mind to do so. And
accordingly she kept very quiet, and took no part, but
inclined silently to her mother's side.

This day was to Dick Cavendish like a bad dream.
He could not move outside the inclosure of the Rectory
grounds without seeing before him in the distance the high
garden wall, the higher range of windows, the big trees
which gave its name to the Elms. Going through the
village street, he saw twice—which seemed a superfluity of
ill-fortune—Lizzie Hampson, with her demure air, passing
without lifting her eyes, as if she had never seen him before.
Had any one else known what he alone knew, how extraordinary would his position have appeared ! But he had
no leisure to think of the strangeness of his position, all
his faculties being required to keep himself going, to look
as if everything was as usual. The terror which was in his
mind of perhaps, for anything he could tell, meeting
some one in these country roads, without warning, to
meet whom would be very different from meeting Lizzie
Hampson, by times got the better of his composure altogether. He did not know what he would do or say in
such an emergency. But he could do nothing to avoid it.
The Wilberforces, anxious to amuse him, drove him over in
the waggonette, in the morning, to Pierrepoint, making a

little impromptu picnic among the ruins. Under no circumstances could the party have been very exciting, except to
the children, who enjoyed it hugely, with the simple appetite
for anything that is supposed to be pleasure which belongs
to their age. They passed the Elms both coming and going.
Mrs. Wilberforce put her parasol between her and that
objectionable house, but all the same made a rapid inspec-
tion of it through the fringes. Dick turned his head away;
but he, too, saw more than any one could be supposed to
see who was looking in the other direction, and at the same
time, with an almost convulsion of laughter, which to himself
was horrible, perceived the double play of curiosity and
repugnance in his hostess with a fierce amusement. He had
to make some sort of poor jest, he did not know what, to
account for the laugh which tore him asunder, which he
could not keep in. What the joke was he did not know,
but it had an unmerited success, and the carriage rattled
along past the garden wall in a perfect riot of laughter from
the fine lungs of the rector and Flo and Georgie and all
the little ones. If any one had but known! The tragedy
was horrible, but the laughter was fresh and innocent on all
lips but his own. Coming back he laughed no more. The
gates were being opened; a sound of horses' hoofs and the
jingle of their furniture was audible. The inhabitants were
about to drive out. " If you look back you may catch

a glimpse of—those people," the rector whispered. But Dick did not look back. The danger made him pale. Had they met face to face, what would have happened? Could he have sat there safe among the innocent children, and made no sign? But when the evening came, and it was time for the dinner at the Warren, he had regained his composure, which, so far as his companions were aware, had never been lost.

In the Warren there were strong emotions, perhaps passions, which he did not understand, but which gave him a sort of fellow-feeling more sympathetic than the well-being of the rector and his wife. Nothing is more pleasant to see than the calm happiness of a wedded pair, who suit each other, who have passed the youthful period of commotion, and have not reached that which so often comes when the children in their turn tempt the angry billows. But there is something in that self-satisfied and self-concentrated happiness which jars upon those who in the turmoil of existence have not much prospect of anything so peaceful. And then domestic comfort is often so sure that nothing but its own virtue could have purchased such an exemption from the ills of life. The Warren had been a few months ago a pattern of humdrum peacefulness. The impatience that sometimes lit up a little fire in Mrs. Warrender's eyes was so out of character, so

improbable, that any one who suspected it believed himself
to have been deceived; for who could suppose the mother
to be tired of her quiet existence? And the girls were
not impatient; they lived their half-vegetable life with the
serenest and most complacent calm. Now, however, new
emotions were at work. The young master of the house
was full of abstraction and dreams, wrapped in some pursuit,
some hope, some absorbing preoccupation of his own. His
mother was straining at her bonds like a greyhound in a
leash. Minnie, who had been the chief example of absolute self-satisfaction and certainty that everything was right,
had developed a keenness of curiosity and censure which
betrayed her conviction that something had gone wrong.
These three were all, as it were, on tiptoe, on the boundary
line, the thinnest edge which divided the known from the
unknown; conscious that at any moment something might
happen which would disperse them and shatter all the re-
mains of the old life.

Chatty alone, amid these smouldering elements of
change, sat calm in her accustomed place as yet un-
awakened except to the mild pleasure of a new face
among those to which she was accustomed, and of a
cheerful voice and laugh which broke the monotony. She
had not even gone so far as to say to herself that such a
cheerful presence coming and going might make life more

interesting. The new-comer, she was quite well aware, was going away to-morrow, nor was there any reason within her power of divination why he should not go ; but he was a pleasant break. Chatty reasoned with herself that though a love of novelty is a bad thing and quite unjustifiable in a woman, still that when something new comes of itself across one's point of vision, there is no harm in taking the good of it. And accordingly she looked up with her face of pleasure, and smiled at the very sound of Dick's cheerful voice, thinking how delightful it must be to be so cheerful as that. What a happy temperament ! If Theo had been as cheerful ! But then to think of Theo as cheerful was beyond the power of mortal imagination. Thus they sat round the table, lighted by a large lamp standing up tall in the midst, according to the fashion of the time. In those days the light was small, not because of æsthetic principles, but because people had not as yet learned how to make more light, and the moderator lamp was the latest invention.

"We took Mr. Cavendish to Pierrepoint, as you suggested," said Mrs. Wilberforce. "We had a very nice drive, but the place is really infested by persons from Highcombe : the woman at the gate told us there had been a party of thirty people from the works the day before yesterday. Sir Edward will soon find the consequences if he goes on in that way. If everybody is allowed to go, not only will they ruin the place, but other people, people like ourselves, will give up going.   He might as well make it a penny show."

"It is a show without the penny," said the rector.

"If the poor people did any harm, he would, no doubt, stop their coming," said Mrs. Warrender mildly.

"Harm! but of course they do harm.   The very idea of thirty working-people, with their heavy boots, and their dinner in a basket, and smoking, no doubt!"

"That is bad," said Dick.   "Wilberforce and I did nothing of that kind.   We only made explorations in the ruins, and used a little tobacco to keep off the bad air. The air in the guard-room was close, and Georgie had a puff at a cigarette, but only with a sanitary view.   And our dinner was in a hamper; there are distinctions.   By the way, it was not dinner at all; it was only lunch."

"And we, I hope, Mr. Cavendish, are very different from——"

"Oh, very different.   We have most things we wish to have, and live in nice houses, and have gardens of our own, and woods to walk in."

"That is quite true," said Minnie; "and we have always been Liberal,—not against the people, as the Conservatives are; but still it cannot be good to teach them to be discontented with what they have.   We should all be contented with what we've got. If it had not been the best for us, it would not have been chosen for us."

"Perhaps we had better not go into the abstract question, Minnie. I suppose, Mr. Cavendish, you go back to Oxford after the vacation?"

"For hard work," he said, with a laugh. "I am such an old fellow I have no time to lose. I am not an honour man, like Warrender."

"And you, Theo,—you are going too?" said the rector.

Warrender woke up as out of a dream. "I have not made up my mind. Perhaps I shall, perhaps not; it is not of much importance."

"Not of much importance!   Your first class——"

"I should not take a first class," he said coldly.

"But, my dear fellow!——" The rector's air of puzzled consternation, and the look he cast round him, as if to ask the world in general for the reason of this extraordinary self-sacrifice, was so seriously comic that Dick's gravity was in danger, especially as all the other members of the party replied to the look with a seriousness, in some cases disapproval, in some astonishment, which heightened the effect.

"Where does he expect to go to?" he said solemnly.

"Theo thinks," said his mother, "that a first class is not everything in the world as it is in the University."

"But my dear Mrs. Warrender! that is precisely one of the things that ladies never understand."

"I have no chance of one, so I agree with Warrender," said Dick. "The Dons will bother, but what does that matter? They have no souls beyond the class lists."

"This is all extremely unnecessary," said Warrender, with an air of suppressed irritation. "Perhaps you will allow me to know best. I have no more chance of a first class than you have, Cavendish. I have not worked for it, and I have no expectation of it. All that was over long ago. I thought every one knew."

"Every one knew that you could have whatever you chose to have, Warrender. Some thought it foolish, and some fine; but every one knew exactly the cause."

"Fine!" said the young master of the house, growing red. "But it is of no consequence to me what they say. I may go back, or I may not; it is not of the slightest importance to any one but myself." He added in a tone which he tried to make lighter, "What use is a class of any kind to a small country gentleman? To know the cost of cultivation and what pays best is better than a dozen firsts. I want to find out how to cut my trees, and how to manage my farmers, and how not to make a fool of myself at petty sessions. Neither Plato nor Aristotle could throw any light on these subjects."

"For the last you must come to me," said Dick; "on that point you'll find me superior to all the sages put together. And as for drawing leases—but I suppose you have some beggar of a man of business who will take the bread out of a poor beginner's mouth."

"Though Mr. Cavendish talks in that way," said Mrs. Wilberforce aside to Minnie, "as though he wanted employment so much, he has a very nice little fortune of his own. It is just his way of talking. And as for connection, there is no one better. His father is a cousin—it may be a good many times removed, but still it is quite traceable—of the Duke. I am not sure, even, that they are not in the Peerage as collaterals; indeed, I am almost sure they are, and that we should find him and everything about him, if we looked."

"Of course everybody knows he is very well connected," said Minnie, "but young men all talk nonsense. Listen to Theo! Why shouldn't he go back to Oxford and take his degree, like other people? I don't care about the class. A gentleman need not be particularly clever; but if he has been at the University and does not take his degree, it is always supposed that there is some reason. I don't think it is respectable, for my part."

"Ah, my dear, the young men of the present day, they are a law to themselves," said her friend. "They don't care for what is respectable. Indeed, so far as I can see, they make it a sort of reproach; they let nobodies pick up the prizes. And what do they expect it is all to end in? I could tell them very well, if they would listen to me. The French Revolution is what it will end in; but of course they will not listen to anything one can say."

"Oh, you know we are Liberals," cried Minnie; "we don't go in with that."

"If you are going to town to-morrow, Cavendish, I don't mind if I go with you," said Warrender. "I have some business to look after. At least, it is not exactly business," for he saw his mother's eyes turned on him inquiringly; "it is a commission from a friend. I shall only stay a night, mother; you need not look so surprised."

"It will do you good," she said quietly. "And why should you hurry back? You will be the better for the change."

He gave her a suspicious, half-angry look, as if he saw more in her words than met the eye. "I shall only be gone a single night," he said.

"I will do all I can to upset his good resolutions, Mrs. Warrender. He shall go to all sorts of notorious places to keep me in countenance. If he can be beguiled into any little improprieties, I am your man."

"Don't be afraid," said the rector. "Dick's wickednesses are all theoretical. I'd trust Georgie in the worst haunt he knows."

Dick looked up with a laugh, with some light word of contradiction, and in a moment there gleamed before him, as by the touching of a spring, as by the opening of a door, the real state of the case so far as he was himself concerned. The present scene melted away to give place to another,— to others which were burnt upon his memory in lines of fire; to one which he could see in his imagination, with which he had a horrible connection, which he could not dismiss out of his thoughts, though he was in reality a fugitive from it, flying the vicinity, the possible sight, the spectre of a ruin which was beyond description. Merely to think of this amid an innocent company, around this decorous table, brought a sickening sensation, a giddiness both mental and physical. He turned his head away from the eyes of the mother, who, he felt, must, in her experience, divine something from the expression in his, to meet the pleased and guileless look with which Chatty was listening to that laughing disclaimer which he had just made. She was sitting by his side, saying nothing herself, listening to the talk, amused and almost excited by the new voice, the little play of light intercourse; even the charm of a new voice was something to Chatty. And she was so certain that what the rector said was true, that Georgie, or even she herself, more delicate still, a simple-hearted young woman, might have been trusted in his worst haunt. He read her look with a keen pang of feelings contradictory, of sharp anguish and a kind of pleasure. For indeed it was true ; and yet—and yet—— Did they but know !

Warrender walked back with the party as far as the Rectory gate. Indeed, so simple was the place, the entire family came out with them, straying along under the thick shade of the trees to the little gate which was nearest the Rectory. It was a lovely summer night, as different as possible from the haze and chill of the preceding one, with a little new moon just disappearing, and everything softened and whitened by her soft presence in the sky. Mrs. Wilberforce and Minnie went first, invisible in the dimness of the evening, then the two solid darknesses of the rector and Warrender. Dick came behind with Mrs. Warrender, and Chatty followed a step in the rear of all. The mother talked softly, more than she had done as yet. She told him that their home henceforward would probably be in Highcombe, not here,—"That is, not yet, perhaps, but soon," she said, with a little eagerness not like the melancholy tone with which a new-made widow talks of leaving her home,—and that it would please her to see him there, if, according to the common formula, "he ever came that way." And Dick declared with a little fervour which was unnecessary that he would surely go, that it would be always a pleasure. Why should he have said it? He had no right to say it; for he knew, though he could not see, with once more that pang of mingled pleasure and misery, that there was a look of pleased satisfaction on Chatty's face as she came softly in the darkness behind.

CHAPTER XV

DICK was astir very early next morning. He did his packing hurriedly, and strolled out in the freshness of the early day. But not to enjoy the morning sunshine. He walked along resolutely towards the house which had suddenly acquired for him so painful an interest. For why? With no intention of visiting it; with a certainty that he would see no one there; perhaps with an idea of justifying himself to himself for flying from its neighbourhood, for putting distance, at least the breadth of the island, between him and that place, which he could not henceforward get out of his mind. To think that he had come here so lightly two days ago with his old uncle's commission, and that now no inducement in the world, except death or hopeless necessity, could induce him to cross that threshold. If the woman were on her death-bed, yes; if she was abandoned by all and without other help, as well might be, as would be, without doubt, one time or another. But for nothing else, nothing less. He walked along under the wall, and round the dark shrubberies behind which enveloped the house. All was quiet and peace, for the moment at least; the curtains drawn over the windows; the household late of stirring; no lively housewife there to rouse maids and men, and stir up a wholesome stir of living. The young man's cheerful face was stern as he made this round, like a sentinel, thinking of many things that were deep in the gulf of the past. Two years of his life which looked like a lifetime, and which were over, with all the horrors that were in them, and done with, and never to be recalled again. He was still young, and yet how much older than any one was aware! Twenty-seven, yet with two lives behind him : one that of youth, to which he had endeavoured to piece his renewed existence; and the other all complete and ended, a tragedy, yet like many tragedies in life, cut off not by death. Not by death, for here were both the actors again within reach of each other, —one within the sleeping house, one outside in the fresh air of the morning,—with a gulf like that between Dives and Lazarus, a gulf which no man might cross, of disgust and loathing, of pain and hatred, between.

The door in the wall opened stealthily, softly, and some one came out. It was so early that such precautions seemed scarcely necessary. Perhaps it was in fear of seeing him, though that was so unlikely, that Lizzie

looked round so jealously. If so, her precautions were
useless, as she stepped out immediately in front of the
passenger whom she most desired to avoid. He did not
speak to her for a moment, but walked on, quickening his
pace as hers fluttered into a run, as if to escape him.
" Stop," he said at length. " You need not take the trouble
to conceal yourself from me."

" I'm not concealing—anything," said Lizzie, half angry,
half sullen, with a flush on her face. " I've done nothing
wrong," she added quickly.

" I don't say you've done anything wrong ; for what I
can tell you may be doing the work of an angel."

She looked up at him eagerly, and the tears sprang to
her eyes. " I don't know for that. I—I don't ask nothing
but not to be blamed."

" Lizzie," he said, " you were always a good girl—and
to be faithful as you seem, may, for anything I know, be
angels' work. I could not do it, for my part."

" Oh no," she said, hurriedly. " It could not be
looked for from you,—oh no, no !"

" But think if you were to ruin yourself," he said.
" The rector saw you the other day, but he will say nothing.
Yet think if others saw you."

" Sir," cried Lizzie, drawing back, " it will do me more
harm and vex granny more to see a gentleman walking by

my side and talking like that, as if he took an interest in me,—which you don't, all the same," she added, with a little bitterness, " only for—others."

" I do," he cried, " if I could help you without harming you. But it is chiefly for the other. I want you to act for me, Lizzie. If trouble should come, as come, of course, it will—— "

" I am none so sure. You never saw her half so pretty —and he——"

" Silence !" cried Dick, with a voice that was like the report of deep guns. " If trouble comes, let me know. She must not want or be miserable. There is my address. Do not apply to me unless there is absolute need ; but if that comes, write, telegraph,—no matter which; help shall come."

" And what am I to do with a gentleman's card ?" said Lizzie. " Granny or some one will be sure to see it. It will drop out of my pocket, or it will be seen in my drawers, or something. And if I were to die it would be found, and folks would think badly of me. I will not take your card."

" This is folly, Lizzie."

" If it is, folly's natural. I don't believe there will be any need ; if there is, I'll find you out, if you're wanted, but I won't take the card. Will you please, sir, to walk on ? I've got my character to think of."

The girl stopped short, leaning against the corner of the wall, defying him, though she was not hostile to him. He put back his card in his pocket, and took off his hat, which was a recognition which brought the colour to Lizzie's cheek.

"Go away, sir; I've got my character to think of," she said. Then she curtsied deeply, with a certain dignity in her rustic manners. "Thank you," she said, "all the same."

Dick walked into the rector's dining-room with little Georgie seated on his shoulder. "Fancy where we found him, mamma," said Flo. "Buying barley sugar from old Mrs. Bagley at the shop. What does a gentleman want with barley sugar? He is too old. You never eat it, nor papa."

"He give it all to me," said Georgie, "and Fluffy had some. Fluffy and me, we are very fond of Mr. Cavendish. Don't go away, Mr. Cavendish, or come back to-morrow."

"Yes, tum back to-morrow," cried the other little ones. Flo was old enough to know that the future had vistas deeper than to-morrow. She said, "Don't be so silly, all you little things. If he was coming back to-morrow, why should he go to-day? He will come back another time."

"When dere's need ob him," said his little godson gravely, at which there was much laughing. But for his part Dick did not laugh. He hid his serious countenance behind little Dick's curly head, and thus nobody knew that there was not upon it even a smile.

At Underwood, which is a very small village, there is no station; so that Dick had to be driven to the railway in the waggonette, the rector making this an occasion to give the children and the governess a drive, so that the two gentlemen could not say much to each other. They had a moment for a last word solely at the door of the railway carriage, in which Warrender had already taken his place. The rector, indeed, had to speak through the carriage window at the last moment. He said, hesitating, "And you won't forget? Tell Mr. Cornwall if he refuses to do anything, so as to drive these people away, it will be the kindest thing he can do for the parish. Tell him——" But here the guard interposed to examine the tickets, and there was a slamming of doors and a shriek of whistles, and the train glided away.

"I think I understand what the rector means," said Warrender. "He is speaking of *that* house. Oh, you need not smile; nothing could be more entirely out of my way."

"I did not smile," said Dick, who was as grave as all the judges in a row.

"Perhaps you have not heard about it. It was there Markland spent the last afternoon before his accident, almost the last day of his life. It gives her a bitter sort of association with the place."

"Markland?" said Dick. "Oh yes, I remember. Lord Markland, who—— He died, didn't he? It may not be a satisfactory household, but still he might have gone there without any harm."

"Oh, I don't suppose there was any harm, except the love of bad company; that seems a fascination which some men cannot resist. I don't care two straws myself whether there was harm or not; but it is a bitter sort of recollection for *her.*"

"They were both quite young, were they not?"

"Markland was over thirty," said the young man, who was but twenty-two; "and she is—oh, she is, I suppose, about my age."

He knew, indeed, exactly what was her age; but what did that matter to a stranger? She was superior to him, it was true, in that as in all other things.

"I have heard they were not very happy," Dick said. He cared no more for the Marklands than he did for the domestic concerns of the guard who had looked at his ticket two minutes ago; but anything answered for conversation, which in the present state of his mind he could not exert himself to make brilliant.

"Oh, happy!" cried Warrender. "How could they

be happy? She a woman with the finest perceptions, and a mind—such as you seldom find in a woman; and he the sort of person who could find pleasure in the conversation that goes on in a house like that."

Dick did not say anything for some time; he felt as though all the people he met in these parts must go on like this, in absolute unconsciousness, giving him blow after blow. "I don't mean to take up the cudgels for that sort of people," he said at last; "but they are—not always stupid, you know." But to this semi-defence his companion gave no heed.

"She was no more than a child when she was married," said Warrender, with excitement, "a little girl out of the nursery. How was she to know? She had never seen any-body, and to expect her to be able to judge at sixteen——"

"That is always bad," said Dick, musing. He was like the other, full of his own thoughts. "Yet some girls are very much developed at sixteen. I knew a fellow once who—— And she went entirely to the bad."

"What are you talking of?" cried Warrender, almost roughly. "She was like a little angel herself, and knew nothing different—and when that fellow—who had been a handsome fellow they say—fell in love with her, and would not leave her alone for a moment, I, for one, forgive her for being deceived. I admire her for it," he went on.

"She was as innocent as a flower. Was it possible she could suspect what sort of a man he was? It has given her such a blow in her ideal that I doubt if she will ever recover. It seems as if she could not believe again in genuine, unselfish love."

"Perhaps it is too early to talk to her about such subjects."

"Too early! Do you think I talk to her about such subjects? But one cannot talk of the greatest subjects as we do without touching on them. Lady Markland is very fond of conversation. She lets me talk to her, which is great condescension, for she is—much more thoughtful, and has far more insight and mental power, than I."

"And more experience," said Dick.

"What do you mean? Well, yes; no doubt her marriage has given her a sort of dolorous experience. She is acquainted with actual life. When it so happens that in the course of conversation we touch on such subjects I find she always leans to the darker side." He paused for a moment, adding abruptly, "And then there is her boy."

"Oh," said Dick, "has she a boy?"

"That's what I'm going to town about. She is very anxious for a tutor for this boy. My opinion is that he is a great deal too much for her. And who can tell what he may turn out? I have brought her to see that he wants a man to look after him."

"She should send him to school. With a child who has been a pet at home that is the best way."

" Did I say he had been a pet at home? She is a great deal too wise for that. Still, the boy is too much for her, and if I could hear of a tutor—— Cavendish, you are just the sort of fellow to know. I have not told her what I am going to do, but I think if I could find some one who would answer I have influence enough——" Warrender said this with a sudden glow of colour to his face, and a conscious glance; a glance which dared the other to form any conclusions from what he said, yet in a moment avowed and justified them. Dick was very full of his own thoughts, and yet at sight of this he could not help but smile. His heart was touched by the sight of the young passion, which had no intention of disclosing itself, yet could think of nothing and talk of nothing but the person beloved.

"I don't know how you feel about it, Warrender," he said, "but if I had a—friend whom I prized so much, I should not introduce another fellow to be near her con-stantly, and probably to—win her confidence, you know ; for a lady in these circumstances must stand greatly in need of some one to—to consult with, and to take little things off her hands, and save her trouble, and—and all that."

"That is just what I am trying to do," said Warrender. "As for her grief, you know—which isn't so much grief as a dreadful shock to her nerves, and the constitution of her mind, and many things we needn't mention—as for that, no one can meddle. But just to make her feel that there is some one to whom nothing is a trouble, who will go anywhere, or do anything——"

"Well: that's what the tutor will get into doing, if you don't mind. I'll tell you, Warrender, what I would do if I were you. I'd be the tutor myself."

"I am glad I spoke to you," said the young man. "It is very pleasant to meet with a mind that is sympathetic. You perceive what I mean. I must think it all over. I do not know if I can do what you say, but if it could be managed, certainly—— Anyhow, I am very much obliged to you for the advice."

"Oh, that is nothing," said Dick; "but I think I can enter into your feelings."

"And so few do," said Warrender; "either it is made the subject of injurious remarks—remarks which, if they came to her ears, would—or a succession of feeble jokes more odious still, or suggestions that it would be better for me to look after my own business. I am not neglecting my own business that I am aware of; a few trees to cut down, a few farms to look after, are not so important. I hope now," he added, "you are no longer astonished that the small interests of the University don't tell for very much in comparison."

"I beg you a thousand pardons, Warrender. I had forgotten all about the University."

"It does not matter," he said, waving his hand; "it does not make the least difference to me. It would not change my determination in any way, whatever might depend upon it; and nothing really depends upon it. I can't tell you how much obliged I am to you for your sympathy, Cavendish." He added, after a moment, "It is doubly good of you to enter into my difficulties, everything being so easy-going in your own life."

Cavendish looked at his companion with eyes that twinkled with a sort of tragic laughter. It was natural for the young one to feel himself in a grand and unique position, as a very young man seized by a *grande passion* is so apt to do; but the fine superiority and conviction that he was not as other men gave a grim amusement to the man who was so easy-going, whose life was all plain sailing in the other's sight. "All the more reason," he said, with a laugh, "being safe myself, that I should take an interest in you." He laughed again, so that for the moment Warrender, with momentary rage, believed himself the object of his friend's derision. But a glance at Cavendish dispelled this fear, and presently each retired into his corner, and they sat opposite to each other saying nothing, while the long levels of the green country flew past them, and the clang of the going swept every other sound away. They were alone in their compartment, each buried in his thoughts : the one in all the absorption of a sudden and overwhelming passion, not without a certain pride in it and in himself, although consciously thinking of nothing but of *her*, going over and over their last interviews, and forming visions to himself of the future ; while the other, he who was so easy-going, the cheerful companion, unexpectedly found to be so sympathetic, but otherwise somewhat compassionately regarded as superficial and commonplace by the youth newly plunged into life,—the other went back into those recollections which were his, which had been confided to none, which he had thought laid to rest and half forgotten, but which had suddenly surged up again with so extraordinary a revival of pain. The presence of Warrender opposite to him, and the unconscious revelation he had made of the condition of his own mind and thoughts, had transported Dick back again for a moment into what seemed an age, a century past, the time when he had been as his friend was, in the ecstasy of a youthful passion. He remembered that; then with quick scorn and disdain turned from the thought, and plunged into the deep abysses of possibility which he now

saw opening at his feet. He had said to himself that the
past was altogether past, and that he could begin in his
own country, far from the associations of his brief and
unhappy meddling with fate, a new existence, one natural
to him, among his own people, in the occupations he
understood. He had not understood either himself or life
in that strange, extravagant essay at living which he had
made and ended, as he had thought, and of which nobody
knew anything. How could he tell, he asked himself
now, how much or how little was known? Was anything ever ended until death had put the finis to mortal
history?

These young men sat opposite to each other, two excellent examples of the well-born, well-bred young Englishman,
admirably dressed, with that indifference to and ease in their
well-fitting garments, that easy and careful simplicity, which
only the Anglo-Saxon seems able to attain to in such
apparel; Warrender, indeed, with something of that dreamy
look about the eyes which betrays the abstraction of the
mind in a realm of imagination, but nothing besides which
could have suggested to any spectator the presence of either
mystery in the past or danger in the future, beyond the
dangers of flood or field. They were both above the reach
of need, but both with that wholesome necessity for doing
which is in English blood, and all the world before them—

public duty and private happiness, the inheritance of the class to which they belonged. Yet to one care had come in the guise of passion ; and the other was setting out upon a second beginning, no one knew how heavily laden and handicapped in the struggle of life.

CHAPTER XVI.

By this time London was on the eve of its periodical moment of desertion; the fashionable people all gone or going; legislators weary and worn, blaspheming the hot late July days, and everything grown shabby with dust and sunshine; the trees and the grass no longer green, but brown in the parks; the flowers in the balconies overgrown; the atmosphere all used up and exhausted; and the great town, on the eve of holiday, grown impatient of itself. Although fashion is but so small a part of the myriads of London, it is astonishing how its habits affect the general living, and how many, diversely and afar off, form a certain law to themselves of its dictates, though untouched by its tide.

Warrender had never known anything about London. His habits were entirely distinct from those of the young men, both high and low, who find their paradise in its haunts and crowds. When he left Cavendish on their arrival, not without a suggestion on Dick's part of an after meeting which the other did not accept, for no reason but

because in his present condition it was more pleasant to
him to be alone, Warrender, who did not know where to
go or what to do in order to carry out the commission
which he had so vaguely taken upon him, walked vaguely
along, carrying about him the same mist of dreams which
made other scenes dim.   Where was he to find a tutor in
the streets of London?   He turned to the Park by habit,
as that was the direction in which, half mechanically, he
was in the habit of finding himself when he went to town.
But he was still less likely to find a tutor for Lady Markland's
boy in the lessened ranks of the loungers in Rotten Row
than he was in the streets.   He walked among them with
his head in the clouds, thinking of what she had said when
last he saw her; inquiring into every word she had uttered;
finding, with a sudden flash of delight, a new meaning
which might perchance lurk in a phrase of hers, and which
could be construed into the intoxicating belief that she had
thought of him in his absence.   This was far more interesting than any of the vague processional effects that glided
half seen before his eyes, the streams of people with no
apparent meaning in them, who were going and coming,
flowing this way and the other, on their commonplace business.   The phantasmagoria of moving forms and faces went
past and past, as he thought, altogether insignificant, meaning nothing.   She had said, " I wondered if you remarked "

—something that had happened when they were apart from
each other; a sunset it was, now he remembered, of
remarkable splendour, which she had spoken of next day.
"I wondered if you remarked," not I wonder, which would
have meant that at that moment she was in the act of
wondering, but I wonder*ed*, in the past, as if, when the
glorious crimsons and purples struck her imagination, and
gave her that high delight which nature can give to the
lofty mind (the adjectives too were his, poor boy), she had
thought of him, perhaps, as the one of all her friends who
was most likely to feel as she was feeling. Poor Warrender
was conscious, with bitter shame and indignation against
himself, that at that moment he was buried in his father's
gloomy library, deep in the shadow of those trees which he
had no longer leisure to think of cutting, and was not so
much as aware that there was a sunset at all; and this he
had been obliged to confess, with passionate regret (since she
had seen it, and given it thus an interest beyond sunset-
tings) : but afterwards recalled, with the tempestuous sudden
joy and misery that seized upon him all at once now.

In the middle of Rotten Row ! with still so many pretty
creatures on so many fine horses cantering past, and even
what was more wonderful, Brunson, that inevitable com-
petitor, the substance of solid success to Warrender's
romance of shadowy glory, walking along with his arm in

that of another scholar, and pointing to the man of dreams who saw them not. " He is working out that passage in the *Politics* that your tutor makes such a pother about," said the other. " Not a bit of it," cried Brunson, " for that would pay." But they gave him credit, at all events, for some classic theme, and not for the discoveries he was making in that other subject which is not classic, though universal ; whereas the only text that entered into his dreams was that past tense, opening up so many vistas of thought which he had not realised before. Was there ever a broken sentence of Aristotle that moved so much the scholar to whom a new reading has suddenly appeared ? There is no limiting the power of human emotion which can flow in almost any channel, but enthusiastic indeed must be the son of learning in whose bosom the difference of the past and the present tense would raise so great a ferment. " I wondered if you remarked." It lit up heaven and earth with new lights to Warrender. He wanted no more to raise his musings into ecstasy. He pictured her standing looking out upon the changing sky, feeling perhaps a loneliness about her, wanting to say her word, but with no one near whose ear was fit to receive it. " I wondered "—and he all the while unconscious, like a dolt, like a clod, with his dim windows already full of twilight, his mossy old trees hanging over him, his back turned, even, could it have penetrated through dead

walls and heavy shade, to the glow in the west! While he
thought of it his countenance too glowed with shame. He
said to himself that never, should he live a hundred years,
would he again be thus insensible to that great and splendid
ceremonial which ends the day. For that moment she had
wanted him, she had need of him: and not even in spirit had
he been at hand, as her knight and servant ought to be.

And all this, as we have said, in the middle of Rotten
Row! He remembered the spot afterwards, the very place
where that revelation had been made to him : but never was
aware that he had met Brunson, who was passing through
London on his way to join a reading party, and was in the
meantime, in passing, making use of all the diversions that
came in his way, in the end of the season, as so reasonable
and practical a person naturally would do.

Warrender went long and far in the strength of this
marvellous supply of spiritual food, and wanted no other;
but at last, a long time after, when it was nearly time to go
back to his train, bethought himself that it would be better
to lunch somewhere, for the sake of the questions which
would be certainly put to him when he got home on this
point. In the meantime he had occupied himself by
looking out and buying certain new books, which he had
either heard her inquire about or thought she would like to
see—and remembered one or two trifles she had mentioned

which she wanted from town, and even laid in a stock of
amusements for little Geoff,—boys' books, suited rather to
his years than to his precocity. About the other and more
serious part of his self-constituted mission Warrender,
however, had done nothing. He had passed one of those
"Scholastic Agencies," which it had been his (vague) intention to inquire at, had paused and passed it by. There
was truth, he reflected, in what Cavendish said. How
could he tell who might be recommended to him as tutor
for Geoff? Perhaps some man who would be his own
superior, to whom she might talk of the sunset or even of
other matters, who might worm his way into the place
which had already begun to become Warrender's place,—
that of referee and executor of troublesome trifles, adviser
at least in small affairs.

He then began to reflect that in all probability a tutor
in the house would be a trouble and embarrassment to
Lady Markland : one who could come for a few hours
every day (and was there not one who would be too happy
of the excuse to wait upon his mistress daily ?) one who
could engage Geoff with work to be done, so that the
mother might be free ; one, indeed, who would thus
supplement the offices already held, and become indis-
pensable where now he was only precariously necessary,
capable of being superseded. It is very possible that

in any case, even had he not asked the valuable advice
of Dick Cavendish, his journey to London would have
come to nothing; for he was in the condition to which a
practical proceeding of such a kind is inharmonious, and
in which all action is somewhat against the grain. But
with the support of Dick's advice his reluctance was justified
to himself, and he returned to Underwood with a consciousness of having given up his first plan for a better one, and
of having found by much thought an expedient better calculated to answer all needs. Meanwhile he carried with him
everywhere the delight of that discovery which he had made.
To say over the words was enough,—I wondered if you
remarked. Had Cavendish been with him on the return
journey, or had any stranger addressed him on the way,
this was the phrase which he would have used in reply.
He watched the sunset eagerly as he walked home from the
station, laden with his parcel of books. It was not this
time a remarkable sunset. It was even a little pale, as if
it might possibly rain to-morrow, but still he watched, with
an eye to all the changes of colour. Perhaps nature had
not hitherto called him with a very strong voice ; but there
came a great many scraps of poetry floating in his head
which might have given an interest to sunsets even before
Lady Markland. There was something about that very
golden greenness which was before his eyes, " beginning to

fade in the light he loves on a bed of daffodil sky." He
identified that and all the rims of colours that marked the
shining horizon. Perhaps she would ask him if he had
remarked; and he would be able to reply.

"Books?" cried Minnie—"are all those books? Don't
you know we have a great many books already, more than
we have shelves for? The library is quite full, and even
the little bookcase in the drawing-room. You should get
rid of some of the old ones if you bring in so many
new."

"And who did you see in town, Theo?" said his
mother. He had no club, being so young and so little
accustomed to London; but yet a young man brought up
as he had been can scarcely fail to have many friends.

"Most people seem to have gone away," he said. "I
saw nobody. Yes, there were people riding in the Row,
and people walking too, I suppose, but nobody I knew."

"And did you go up all that way only to buy books?
You might have written to the bookseller for them, and
saved your fare."

Theo made his sister no reply, but when Chatty asked,
rather shyly, if he had seen much of Mr. Cavendish, answered
warmly that Cavendish was a very good fellow; that he took
the greatest interest in his friends' concerns, and was always
ready to do anything he could for you. "I had no idea

what a man he was," he said, with fervour. Mrs. Warrender looked up at this with a little anxiety, for according to
the ordinary rules which govern the reasoning of women
she was led from it to the deduction, not immediately visible
to the unconcerned spectator, that her son had got into
some scrape, and had found it necessary to have recourse
to his friend's advice. Theo in a scrape! It seemed
impossible : but yet there are few women who are not prepared for something happening of this character even to
the best of men.

"I hope," she said, "that he is a prudent adviser, Theo;
but he is still quite a young man."

"Not so young; he must be six or seven and twenty,"
said the young man; and then he paused, remembering that
this was the perfect age,—the age which she had attained,
which he had described to Cavendish as "about my own,"
—and he blushed a little and contradicted himself. "Yes,
to be sure, he is young: but that makes him only the more
sympathetic; and it was not his advice I was thinking of so
much as his sympathy. He is full of sympathy."

"You have us to sympathise with you," said Minnie.
"I don't know what you want from strangers. We ought
to stand by each other, and not care what outsiders say."

"I hope Theo will never despise the sympathy of his
own people, but—a friend of your own choosing is a great

help," said Mrs. Warrender. Yet she was uneasy. She did not think young Cavendish's sympathy could be on account of Theo's late bereavement, and what trouble could the boy have that he confided to Cavendish, and did not mention to his mother? She became more and more convinced that there must be some scrape, or at least that something had gone wrong. But save in these speeches about Cavendish there was no proof of anything of the kind. He gave no further explanation, however, of the business which had taken him to town, unless the fact that he drove over to Markland next morning with the half of the pile of books which he had brought from town, in his dog-cart, should afford an explanation; and that was so vague that it was hard to say what it did or did not prove.

He went over to Markland with his books, but left them in the dog-cart, shy, when he was actually in her presence, of carrying her that bribe. Books were a bribe to her; she had been out of the way of gratifications of this kind, and too solitary and forsaken during the latter part of her married life to know what was going on and to supply herself. She was sitting with Geoff upon the terrace, which ran along one side of the house, when Warrender appeared, and both teacher and pupil received him with something that looked very like relief; for the day was warm, and the terrace was but ill chosen as a schoolroom. The infinite

charm of a summer day, the thousand invitations to idleness
with which the air is full, the waving trees (though there
were not many of them), the scent of the flowers, the singing of the birds, all distracted Geoff's attention, and sooth
to say his mother's too.   She would have been glad to sit
quiet, to escape the boy's questioning, to put away the
irksome lessons which she herself did not much more than
understand, and to which she brought a mind unaccustomed
and full of other thoughts.   Of these other thoughts there
were so many, both of the future and the past : it was very
hard to keep her attention to the little boy's Latin grammar.
And Geoff on his side was weary too; he should have been
in a schoolroom, shut out from temptation, with maps
hung along the walls, instead of waving trees, and where he
could not have stopped to cry out, " I say, mamma, there's
a squirrel.   I am certain it is a squirrel," in the midst of
his exercises.   That, of course, was very bad.   And then
up to a recent period he had shared all, or almost all, his
mother's thoughts; but since his father's death these had
become so full of complications that a child could no longer
share them, though neither quite understood the partial
severance which had ensued.   Both were relieved, however,
when the old butler appeared at the end of the terrace,
pointing out to Warrender where the little group was.   The
man did not think it necessary to expose himself to the full

blaze of the sunshine in order to lead "a great friend" like
Mr. Warrender close up to my lady's chair.

"We are very glad to see you; in fact, we are much
too glad to see you," said Lady Markland, with a smile.
"We are ashamed to say that we were not entering into
our work as we ought. Nature is always so busy doing a
hundred things, and calling us to come and look what she
is about. We take more interest in her occupations than
in our own."

"Mamma makes a story of everything," said Geoff, half
aggrieved; "but I'm in earnest. Grammar is dreadful stuff;
there are no reflections in it. Why can't one begin to read
books straight off, without nasty, stupid rules?"

Warrender took little note of what the boy said. Meanwhile he had shaken hands and made his salutations, and
his sovereign lady, with a smile, had given him a chair.
He felt himself entering, out of the blank world outside,
into the sphere of her existence, which was his Vita Nuova,
and was capable for the moment of no other thought.

"I think," said Lady Markland,—"for we have really
been at it conscientiously for a long time and doing our
best,—I think, Geoff, we may shut up our books for to-day.
You know there will be your lessons to prepare to-night."

"I'll go and look at Theo's horse. Have you got that
big black one? I shall be back in a moment, mamma."

"If you look behind you will find some books, Geoff; some that perhaps you will like."

"Oh, good!" said the boy, with his elfish little countenance lighting up. He was very slight and small for his age, a little shadow darting across the sunshine. The half of the terrace lay in a blaze of light, but all was cool and fresh in the corner where Lady Markland's light chairs and table were placed in the angle of the balustrade, there half hidden by a luxuriant climbing rose. Above Lady Markland's head was a cluster of delicate golden roses, tinged in their hearts with faint red, in all the wealth of their second bloom. Her black dress, profound black, without any relief, was the only dark point in the scene. A little faint colour of recovering health, and perhaps of brightening life, had come to her face. She was very tranquil, resting as people rest after a long illness, in a sort of convalescence of the heart.

"You must forgive his familiarity, Mr. Warrender; you are so good to him, and at his age one is so apt to presume on that."

Warrender had no inclination to waste the few minutes in which he had her all to himself in any discussion of Geoff. He said hastily, "I have brought some other books to be looked at,—things which people are talking of. I don't know if you will care for them, but there is a little novelty in them, at least. I was in town yesterday——"

" You are very good to me too," she said. "A new book is a wonderful treat. I thought you must be occupied or absent that we did not see you here."

Again that past tense, that indication that in his absence —— Warrender felt his head grow giddy with too much delight. " I was afraid to come too often, lest you should think me—importunate."

" How so ?" she said simply. " You have been like a young brother ever since—— How could I think you other than kind ? The only thing is that you do too much for me. I ought to be trying to walk alone."

" Why, while I am here ?" cried the young man ; " asking nothing better, nothing half so good as to be allowed to do what I can,—which, after all, is nothing."

She gave a slight glance at him under her eyelids, with a faint dawning of surprise at the fervour of his tone. " The world which people say is so hard is really very kind," she said. " I never knew till now how kind—at least when one has a great evident claim upon its sympathy,—or pity, should I say ? Those who find it otherwise are perhaps those whose troubles cannot be made public, and yet who expect their fellow-creatures to divine."

Warrender was sadly cast down to be considered only as the world, a type, so to speak, of mankind in general, kind to those whose claims were undeniable. He replied with a swelling heart, "There must always be individuals who divine, though perhaps they may not dare to show their sympathy,—ah, don't say pity, Lady Markland!"

"You humour me," she said, "because you know I love to talk. But pity is very sweet; there is a balm in it to those who are wounded."

"Sympathy is better.

> " ' Mighty love would cleave in twain
> The lading of a single pain,
> And part it, giving half to him.' "

"Ah," she cried, with a glimmer in her eyes, "if you go to the poets, Mr. Warrender! And that is more than sympathy. What did he call it himself? ' Such a friendship as had mastered time.' "

"Mamma, mamma, look here!" came in advance of his appearance the voice of Geoff. He came panting, flying round the other angle of the terrace, with his arms full of books. And here, as if it were a type of all that was coming, the higher intercourse, the exchange of thought, the promotion of the man over the child, came suddenly to an end.

CHAPTER XVII.

LADY MARKLAND had recovered in a great degree from the shock of her husband's death. It had been, as Mrs. Warrender said, a shock rather than a sorrow. There is no such reconciler of those who have been severed, no such softener of the wounds which people closely connected in life so often give to each other, as death. A long illness ending so has often the effect of blotting out altogether the wrongs and bitternesses of many troubled years. The unkind husband becomes once more a hero, the child who has stung its parents to the quick a young and tender saint, by that blessed process. Nor when death comes in a moment is it of less avail. The horror, the pity, the intolerable pang of sympathy, with which we realise what the sudden end must have been to him who met it, without time to think, without time to repent, without a moment to prepare himself for that incalculable change, affects every mind, even that of the merest spectator; how much more that of one whom the victim had left a few hours before with a careless word, perhaps an insult, perhaps a jest! What changes of mood, what revelations, what sudden adaptation to the supreme necessity, may come with the blow, the spectator, even if he be nearest and dearest to the sufferer, cannot know. He knows only what was and is, and his soul is overwhelmed with pity. In that moment those who are most deeply injured forgive and forget. They remember the time when all was well,— the sweet childhood, the blooming youth, the first love, the halcyon days before trouble came.

Lady Markland had felt this universal influence. But when she showed her husband's portrait to Mrs. Warrender, it was not so much with a renewal of love as with a great anguish of pity that her mind was filled. This for a time veiled even in her mind the relief, which was not altogether to be ignored even then, but which gradually gained upon her, yet still with great gravity and pain. She was free from a bondage which had become intolerable to her, which day by day she had felt herself less able to bear; but this gain was at his cost. To gain anything at the cost of another is painful to a generous mind; but to gain at such a price,—the price as seemed not only of another's life, but of a life to which it had seemed almost impossible that there could be any harmonious completion or exten-sion! For what could he do in another world, in a world of spirits? He had been all fleshly; nothing in him that was not of the earth. In the majority of cases it is a hard thing to understand how a spirit, formed apparently for nothing but the uses of earth, should be able to adapt itself in a moment to those occupations and interests which are congenial to another state of existence; and with young Lord Markland this was peculiarly the case. He had seemed to care for nothing except things which he could not carry with him into the unseen. Had other capacities, other desires, developed in a moment into the new life? This is a question which no one could answer, and his wife could only think of him as he had been. There seemed nothing but suffering, deprivation, for him, in such a change. The wind, when it blew wildly of nights, seemed to her like the moan of a wandering spirit trying vainly to get back to the world which it understood, to the pleasures of which it was capable. And had she bought relief and freedom by such a sacrifice exacted from another? When comforters bid her believe that he had gone to a better place, that it was her loss but his gain,—which in all probability is true in all cases, not only in those of the saints whose natural home is heaven,—her heart rose against them, and contradicted them, though she said nothing. It was—alas that it should be so!—her gain. She dared not, even to herself, deny that; but how could it be his—a man who had no thought but of the beggarly elements of life, no aspiration beyond its present enjoyments? and it was by this dreadful overturn in his existence, this taking from him of everything he cared for, that she had been made free. Such a thought as this is more terrible than sorrow, it is sadder than death. It left her for a long time very grave, full of something which was almost remorse, as if she had done it; wondering whether God himself could make up to poor Geoffrey, who had never thought of Him, for the loss of everything which he had ever thought of or cared for. She could not confide this thought to any spiritual guide,—and indeed she was not a woman to whom a spiritual guide was possible. Her problems, her difficulties, remained in her own breast, where she worked them out as she could, or, perhaps, in process of time, forgot them, which, in the darkness of human understanding, was probably the better way.

But in one respect he had been just, nay, generous, to his wife. He had left the burdened estates, the no-money, the guardianship of her child, entirely to her. His old uncle, indeed, was associated with her in that guardian-ship; but this was merely nominal, for old John Markland was very indifferent, more interested in his own comforts than in all the children in the world, and had no mind to interfere. She found herself thus not only a free woman,

but with what was equal to a new profession upon her
shoulders,—the care of her boy's fortune and of considerable
estates, though at the moment in as low a condition and as
badly managed as it was possible for estates to be.   It was
not the fault of Mr. Longstaffe, who had all the business
of the county in his hands, and who had tried in vain to
save from incumbrance the property which Lord Markland
had weighed down almost beyond redemption.   Mr. Longstaffe, indeed, when he heard of the fatal accident to his
client, had been unable to refrain from a quick burst of
self-congratulation over a long minority, before he composed his countenance to the distress and pity which were
becoming such an occasion.   When the funeral was over,
indeed, he permitted himself to say piously that, though
such an end was very shocking, it was an intervention of
Providence for the property, which could not have stood
another year of Lord Markland's going-on.   He was a
little dubious of Lady Markland's wisdom in taking the
burden of the business upon her own shoulders ; but on the
whole he respected her and her motives, and gave her all
the help in his power.   And Lady Markland let no grass
grow under her feet.   She began proceedings at once with
an energy which nobody had expected from her.   The
horses were sold, and the establishment reduced without
any delay.   The two other houses, both expensive,—the

villa in the Isle of Wight, the shooting-box in the Highlands, —both of which had been necessary to Lord Markland's pursuits, were let as soon as it was possible to secure tenants. And Geoff and his mother began, in one wing of the big barracks at Markland, a life not much different from their past life, except in so far that it was free from interruption and anxiety. The pang of loss in such a case does not last; and Lady Markland entered with all the zest of an active-minded and intelligent woman into the work from which she had been debarred all her previous life. No man, perhaps,—seeing that men can always find serious occupation when they choose to do so,—can throw himself with the same delight into unexpected work as such a woman can do, a woman to whom it is salvation from many lesser miseries, as well as an advantage in itself. She had known nothing hitherto, except that everything was going badly, and that she was helpless to interfere, to arrest the ruin which stared them in the face. And now to feel that she might stop that ruin, might even make up for all the losses of the past, and place her son in the position his father had lost, was a happiness beyond description, and gave new life and exhilaration to all her thoughts.

This change, however, occasioned other changes, which marked the alteration from the old life to the new with difficulties and embarrassments which were inevitable. One of those, and the most important, has been already indicated. It concerned Geoff. The change in Geoff's existence was great. Into the morning-room, where his mother and he had constantly sat together, where he had his lessons, where all the corners were full of his toys, where his little life had been spent from morning till night in such a close and absorbing companionship as can only exist between a parent and an only child, there suddenly intruded things and thoughts with which Geoff had little to do. First came a large writing table, occupying the centre of the room, with all sorts of drawers full of papers, and so many letters and notes and account-books that Geoff looked with astonishment, mingled with awe and admiration, at the work which went on upon it. " Did you write all these ?" he said to his mother, touching with a finger a pile of letters. He was proud of the achievement, without remembering that he had himself sat very forlorn all the morning, in the light of the great bow windows, with his lesson books, and had asked a great many questions, without more response than a smile and a " Presently, dear," from the mother who was generally so ready to meet and reply to every word he said. Geoff kept his place in the window, as he had always done, and after Lady Markland had got through her morning's work there would be an attempt at the lessons, which heretofore had been the pleasant occupation of the whole morn-

ing,—a delightful dialogue, in which the mind of the teacher
was as much stimulated as that of the pupil, since Geoff
conducted his own education by means of a multitude of
questions, to which it was not always very easy to reply.
Under the new *regime*, however, this long process was not
possible, and the lessons had to be said in a summary
manner which did not at all suit Geoff's way of thinking.
He did not complain, but he was puzzled, turning it over
in his mind with slow but progressive understanding. The
big writing-table seemed typical to Geoff. It threw a deep
shadow behind it, making the thick, light-coloured, much-
worn carpet, on which he had trotted all his life, dark and
gloomy, like the robbers' cave he had often found so much
difficulty in inventing in the lightness of the room. He
had a robbers' cave to his desire now in the dark, dark
hole between the two lines of drawers; but it was dearly
bought.

Geoff, however, without being as yet quite clear in his
mind as to his grievance, had instinctively taken what
means were in his power to make up for it. There was
that robbers' cave, for one thing, which had many dramatic
possibilities. And he was a boy who took a great interest
in his fellow-creatures, and liked to listen to talk, especially
when it was of a personal character. He was delighted to
be there, notwithstanding the strange silence to which he

was condemned, when Dickinson, the bailiff, came in to
make his report and to receive his orders. Geoff took the
greatest interest in Dickinson's long-winded stories about
what was wanted in the village, the cottages that were tumbling
to pieces, the things that must be done for the farmers.
Lady Markland was at first greatly amused and delighted
to see how her boy entered into everything, and even made
a gentle boast that Geoff understood better than she did.
It was only when Mr. Longstaffe and her clergyman simul-
taneously snubbed her that this foolish woman came to
herself. Mr. Longstaffe said, in his brusque way, that he
thought Master Geoff—he begged his pardon, little Lord
Markland—would be better at his lessons; while Mr.
Scarsdale put on a very grave air, and remarked that he
feared Dickinson might have things to tell his mistress
which were not fit for a little boy's ears. This last address
had disconcerted the young mother sadly, and cost her
some tears; for she was as innocent as Geoff, and the idea
that there were in the village things to tell her that were
unfit for the child's ears threw her into daily terror, not
only for him, but for herself. This was one of the things
that made it apparent that a new rule was necessary. Her
business grew day by day, as she began to understand it
better, and the lessons fell more and more into the background. Geoff was the soul of loyalty, and did not com-

plain. He developed a quite new faculty of silence, as he sat at his table in the window, now and then stealing a glance at her to see if she were free. That little figure, seated against the light, was all that Lady Markland had to cheer her, as she set out upon this new and stony path of life. He represented everything that made her task possible and her burden grateful to her. Without him always there in the background, what, she asked herself, would existence be to her? She asked herself this question when it first began to be suggested by her friends that Geoff should be sent to school. It is one special feature in the change and downfall that happens to a woman when she becomes a widow that all her friends find themselves at liberty to advise her. However bad or useless her husband may be, so long as he lives she is safe from this exercise of friendship; but when he is dead all mouths are opened. Mr. Scarsdale paid her a visit solemnly, in order to deliver his soul in this respect. "I came on purpose," he said, as if that was an additional virtue, "to speak to you, dear Lady Markland, very seriously about Geoff." And whether it was by his own impulse, or because he was written to on the subject, and inspired by zealous friends nearer home, old Mr. Markland wrote to his dear niece in the same strain, assuring her that it would be far the best thing to send him to school. To school! Her little delicate boy, not nine till April, who had never been out of his mother's care! Lady Markland suffered a great deal from these attacks, and she tried hard, by getting up early, by sitting up late, to find time for Geoff, as of old; but Geoff himself had fallen into the new ways, and the lessons languished. What was she to do?

And then it was that the alternative of a tutor was suggested to her. A tutor! That did not seem so terrible. She confided her troubles to Warrender, who had fallen into the way of riding over to Markland two or three times a week, of checking Dickinson's accounts for her, and looking up little bits of law as between landlord and tenant, and doing his best to make himself necessary; not with any deep-laid plan, but only because to be near her, and serve her, was becoming more and more the desire of his life. Warrender was not fond of Geoff. It is possible, indeed, that his spirits rose with a sense of relief at the suggestion of sending that inevitable third in all their interviews away; but he was at that stage when the wish of a person beloved is strong enough in a young mind to make all endurance possible, and to justify the turning upside down of heaven and earth. He had replied boldly that there would be nothing more easy than to find a tutor; that he himself would go to town, and make inquiries; and that she need contemplate the other dreadful alternative no more. Lady Markland was more grateful to Theo than words could

say, and she told all her friends, with a serene countenance,
that she had made up her mind to the tutor. It is a great
thing to have made up one's mind. It gave a satisfaction
and calm to her spirits that nothing else could have done.
Indeed, she was so satisfied that she avoided the subject
thereafter, and said nothing more to Warrender, who had
constituted himself her agent, and took great care not to
question him about what he had been doing in London,
when she heard that he had been there. For after all, to
come to a determination is the great thing. The practical
part may be put in operation at any moment. What is
really necessary is to make up one's mind.

Something of the same feeling moved Warrender when
he returned from that expedition to London, which has
been already recorded. Dick Cavendish's suggestion had
been to him a suggestion from heaven. But when he
returned home, and as he began to think, there were a
great many secondary matters to be taken into account.
He began to realise the interest that would be taken by the
entire county in a matter which did not concern them in
the very least. He realised the astonished look of his
mother, and felt already his ear transfixed by Minnie's per-
sistent "Why?" Theo saw all these hindrances by degrees.
He said to himself, indignantly, that it was nobody's business
but his own, and that he hoped he was able to judge for

himself. But these reflections do not make an end of a
difficulty ; they only show more distinctly a consciousness
of it. And thus it was that he put off making to Lady
Markland the proposal he intended to make, just as she, on
her side, put off asking him whether he had done anything
in the matter. In the meantime, while the summer lasted,
there were many reasons and excuses for putting off from
day to day.

END OF VOL. I.